SWEET WHISPERS, BROTHER RUSH

SWEET WHISPERS, BROTHER RUSH

Virginia Hamilton

PHILOMEL BOOKS

Grateful acknowledgement to Guin Hillman, R.N., Director of Quality Assurance, Community Hospital, Springfield, Ohio, for her careful scrutiny of hospital procedures and patient admittance and care as depicted in this manuscript.

The author and publishers also acknowledge with thanks permission received from Little, Brown & Co., Boston, and Harold Matson Co., Inc., New York, to quote from pages 57, 58 and 59 of *The Cool World* by Warren Miller, copyright © 1959 by Warren Miller.

Library of Congress Cataloging in Publication Data
Hamilton, Virginia.
    Sweet Whispers, Brother Rush.
    Summary: Fourteen-year-old Tree, resentful of her working mother who leaves her in charge of a retarded brother, encounters the ghost of her dead uncle and comes to a deeper understanding of her family's problems.
    [1. Family problems—Fiction.   2. Single-parent family—Fiction.   3. Ghosts—Fiction]   I. Title.
PZ7.H1828Sw   1982   [Fic]   81-22745
ISBN 0-399-20894-1   AACR2

10   9   8

For my family

SWEET WHISPERS, BROTHER RUSH

CHAPTER

1

The first time Teresa saw Brother was the way she would think of him ever after. Tree fell head over heels for him. It was love at first sight in a wild beating of her heart that took her breath. But it was a dark Friday three weeks later when it rained, hard and wicked, before she knew Brother Rush was a ghost.

That first time Tree didn't notice that it was odd the way Brother happened to be there. He had been standing on a corner of Race Street the way the dudes will do after school, whether they went to school or not. He was standing cool, waiting for whatever would happen to happen, just the way all the dudes did. Tree had come swinging around the corner of Race Street at Detroit Avenue on her way home. She was holding her books tight to her chest, hiding herself from the dudes. She had begun growing into a woman, which was the reason the dudes had started to catcall to her:

"Hey, little girl, when you going to let me take you *out*?"

"Sweet Tree, I'll walk you home, bay-buh. Do Dab know you walkin by these shifless clowns *alone*? Do your brother leave you in the house by you-sef?"

"Shu-man, you know Dab n'goin nowhere, and Tree comin home from schoo."

"I'll brang you home, Teresa, since you gone and grown so fine."

Tree felt so ashamed of them, ashamed they had to go pick on her. One or two of them were quick to understand she wasn't ready for them.

"Stop it, yo'w," they told the others. "She ain cooked good yet." And laughed about it.

Tree knew they weren't bad dudes.

Be never having nothing to do and nowhere to do it, she had thought.

They laughed and joked so much to keep back that fear look — Tree had seen it — from showing through the hard glinting of their hungry eyes.

It was when Tree was almost by them and they had stopped their calling after her that she had spied Brother Rush. He had been leaning on a stoop of an apartment building. She didn't have time to think about the fact that he was off by himself, although she made note of it. The other dudes didn't so much ignore him as they seemed to have forgotten about him. They acted like they didn't even know him or hadn't paid attention that he had come to lean there.

Tree saw him at once. It was the way you see something that has been there all of the time, but you never had eyes open wide enough to see. It was like the figure of him jumped right out of space at her. Brother Rush hit her in one never-to-be-forgotten impression:

His suit was good enough for a funeral or a wedding. Better than a suit for Sunday church or one for Thanksgiving. It was just too dressy for a school concert when you have the main solo. You have been paid thirty-five bills to sing because you are a home boy, a graduate of the school who has done all right and has come on back as an example for the rest of the dudes. Dudes who will not yet admit that they will never leave Race Street or Detroit Avenue, either, although they know they won't. They do know, now.

The suit was dark and rich-looking, pinstripe perfection. The shirt was ivory with a shiny sword design that gave it more class than any shirt Tree had ever seen. The collar was uncrushed around Brother Rush's neck, but not so tight so that it bothered his Adam's apple. His tie was deep wine-dark, and silky. The belt he wore was black and the buckle was silver, and spelled *"Jazz"* in the prettiest script. That convinced Tree he was a musician, and she decided he was a piano player. Brother's shoes were black patent leather dress shoes with a high gloss, which he wore over gray silk socks.

As far as Tree could tell that first time, Brother Rush's clothes were picture perfect. She imagined his underwear. He'd have on a snow-white undershirt with short sleeves; soft-cottony shorts. Nothing like her brother Dab's Fruit-of-the-Loom with ratty tears. Brother's underwear would have no worn-through places.

She hadn't realized that it was the message out of Brother's eyes that had caught her, had captured her. It had all happened too fast. She had the impression of unbelievable good looks—tallness, slimness, those funeral clothes she'd never seen on any dude. Not even the ones into criminality dressed like Brother Rush, the ones who strutted flash-smart and pimp-fine, as her Muh Vy said, upper lip curling.

Tree understood that the way Brother Rush was dressed expressed his style as well as his melancholy. She made fleeting notice that Brother's skin was a pale brown with a good sprinkling of reddish freckles. He had refined features and full lips. His large nose was long, straight, with flared nostrils. His hair had the same reddish tint of the freckles, soft and tightly curled. And he wore suede gloves. She summed up her impression of him as absolutely handsome. His was an appearance of trim, muscular maleness, including his eyes. She denied

11

the message that was there in his eyes. It had gone too deeply inside her for her to fathom it at once. Even so, his eyes had taken her prisoner.

Rush stood on the corner against a stoop with his legs crossed at the ankles. His right hand was cupped around his ear, as if he'd been singing along with some tough do-wahs of an outta-sight 1950s reissue and getting the background whisperings right in tune as well. Or else he had the whole record in his head and was using his hand to his ear to close out street sounds while he hummed the tune. Tree was certain she heard him whispering. His left hand was propped under his right elbow.

The stone finest dude Tree had ever seen in her short life of going-on fifteen years. She didn't say anything to him. What was there to say? He knew he was fine. She knew it. She held her books and looked straight on as she went by him. Brother Rush seemed not to notice her passing by right before his eyes. His head never moved; he stared steadily into Race Street. She knew he had to be scoping on her the way she had scoped on him as she passed. Her insides had performed a wild screeching at her, like a girl swooning in some fifties movie clip she had seen on TV. Brother Rush had to belong to her. She belonged to him the moment she saw him.

Him standing in the street was Tree's very first sighting of Brother. She didn't tell anyone about him. Not her mother, who was Viola, whom they called Muh Vy. Muh Vy, spoken M'Vy, with the softest sighing to mean, Miss you, Mama; Love you, Mama. All the tenderness and grief she and her brother Dab felt at the thought of her when they were so alone sometimes without her. Sighing in their minds, M'Vy! M'Vy!, a stirring of memories, like leaves lifting, swirling on a hot, sudden breeze.

Tree didn't tell Dab about Brother Rush. There were

12

days when Dab was home for her when she got home. He liked being home for her. He'd walk out of school early. There were times when they locked up the school so nobody could walk out. But her brother, Dab, would grow restless enough to find ways to get out. It was best for him that he get out of there when he felt he had to leave. But she didn't tell him.

Don't really know if he home cause he like being home for me, she thought. Think he home cause he don't have no place else to go, Dab don't, the same as me. He wouldn't know where else to go. He do care about me, probably, but that ain't why he come home.

His name was Dabney and everybody called him Dab. Dab this and Dab that. There was not a soul who had anything against Dab. No one in school, including the teachers, thought mean of him. Being almost fifteen, she knew why. Her brother wasn't a basketball star, or the smartest person. No way was Dab the smartest dude around. He never got in any trouble. He never woofed on other dudes or anybody. He would never open his mouth in classes. Dab didn't bring home report cards. Tree and M'Vy wouldn't expect him to.

"Be happy he off the streets," M'Vy say. "Streets n'got nothin to tell a brother, him."

Dab could no more deal with the hype of the street corners than he could work with opening his mouth in school.

It was all right between her and Dab. He was seventeen and he wasn't smart. There. She'd thought it. Some days his head hurt him so bad, he never got off the couch in the living room, lying there in his ratty robe, curled in a ball. Saying that whenever light gets on certain places on his arms, it made him feel like he would jump out of his skin.

"Dab ain't smart. No way," Tree would say when she

13

was by herself in her room or taking off her boots in the foyer. She wouldn't say it to anyone else. But she and Dab knew. She helped him with the countries out of his world history book. Dab had no trouble understanding continents, but all those little countries gave him a headache. Tree helped him with math work. He had taken math for two years, the easiest, commercial math, and it hadn't done him any good. She gave him a calculator she talked M'Vy into buying him one Christmas. Gave the little thing to him as a present, hoping desperately it would help him. It just upset him. He couldn't find the figures that had to go into it to get the answers out.

But Tree loved Dab. When she felt something was missing and she didn't know what it was, she'd go by Dab where he sat to lean on his shoulder. He'd move his head until their foreheads touched. That would last a minute. Then he would put his hands on his forehead and then hold them over his eyes.

There they'd be in the house, so quiet. She'd take a deep breath and feel Dab breathe out in short bursts, like gasps of hurt. She would feel something missing from the house. Dab wouldn't mind her leaning on him. Sometimes he'd take hold of her hand and pat it in some kind of formal, gentlemanly way. Most of the time, though, when it was too quiet, he would have his hands over his eyes. But Tree didn't tell him about Brother Rush the first time she had seen him.

The next time Tree saw Brother, she fell more in love with him. He was standing on the avenue; and again, she did not speak to him. This time she noticed that his standing position might be out of the ordinary. Yet the bold sight of him swept away any worry. He was just there. Not every day; he seemed to be there one day one week and one day the next. Finally she did tell Dab and Dab smiled about it, not saying much. Dab had been busy right then. She could have picked a better time to tell him, instead of all of a sudden saying, "Dab, there's this guy I know—I like him fine."

That didn't tell the whole truth, the loving truth, about how she felt at all. Dab had had this new girl with him. He had lots of girls he brought home. To look at him, he was good-looking almost to pretty. Some girls liked that. But none of them lasted long. Or else Dab didn't last long with them. Whichever way it was, he would bring one home, and another and another after them.

Tree didn't see him bring girls home because he got home early when he left school early, or he would go out and bring them in at night after supper when she had gone to her room. When they didn't watch television, she and Dab had a habit of going off to their separate rooms. If Dab wasn't up in the morning by the time she was ready for school, she would have to go in and wake him up.

Knock on his door and then go in and say, "Dab. Dab." Wake him up and never scare him, either.

If she said *Dab* too loud as she would do if she forgot, it could get awful in that room. It could scare Dab half to death. He'd jump a foot up off the bed. It didn't matter whether a girl was there. Still asleep, he would start swinging. Running. Once he almost ran out the window. And when she had grabbed his arm to save him, he had swung on her and knocked her off her feet. Didn't hurt her, but it scared her.

The only time Dab was ready to fight with you was when you woke him up too fast. If Tree had to go in and wake him, she was likely to find one of his girls there in the bed with him. And she would say to him, "Dab. Dab," very quietly.

Dab would open his eyes just when she thought he

15

wasn't going to hear her. Opening his eyes all of a sudden, staring at her, cold and alert. "Yeah, I hear you, baby Tree." Then the sweet emptiness would swim in a bright stream back into his eyes again, and he would say to the girl, "Bay-buh, bay-buh, tam to go. Uh-huh."

The girl would be awake. When you are not familiar with a place, you wake up as soon as somebody steps into the room. Tree could tell the girl, the woman, was awake with her eyes closed by the way she held herself board stiff and still under the covers. This one was older than Dab and liked him because of that sweet, empty look that could take over his eyes, and because he was young and so pretty.

Tree would leave the room and get ready to go to school. Then Dab would get up. He'd miss the first period of the morning two or three times a week because there would be someone overnight with him. And when Tree got home from school again, the girl might still be there.

Once in a great while, Dab would bring one home after a regular schoolday. Tree would get home first. Then the girl would come in the house with Dab and see Tree, and Tree would hear them talking off in the kitchen.

Hear the girl saying to Dab, "Why you baby-sittin her for? She can stay by her sel, shu, she almost fifteen years old. You don't have to hold her han. That not your job, man. That be her mama's job. She got a mama, hasn't she?"

Dab wouldn't say much. Looking at the girl with his sad, simple eyes. Smile at her, and knowing Tree had heard it all. That would be the last time Tree would see that particular girl. After saying something like that, Dab got rid of them. Always.

So it was Tree and Dab, together most of the time. M'Vy was away for a lot of reasons. She worked; she lived in at people's houses. She was into practical nursing. She made side bets on the street having to do with the daily lottery. Vy loved the *Dream Book Almanac: Numerology Encyclopedia*. Sometimes, she dreamed lucky. M'Vy lived in a patient's house — Tree didn't know how many different patients and houses — and might be gone for weeks at a time. She would come by to Tree and Dab on a Saturday. She'd have money.

And say, "Come on, Tree. Dab, you stay still, we gone brang you back a goody."

They'd get on the bus and buy enough food and goodies to last a month. Store it. Every kitchen cupboard full to the brim with food and goodies.

Tree must have said to M'Vy when she was younger, "Whyn't you home?"

And probably cried about that. But she didn't really remember. She didn't cry now because she was used to the way things were and knew they were the way they had to be. M'Vy had to be somewhere else so she and Dab and M'Vy, too, could have all the things they had to have. She supposed that M'Vy was gone some of the time for her own pleasure. But Tree didn't think too much about that. She accepted M'Vy as mood and background of her life. Muh was the color and shade of shadows that were always in the house. Tree could depend on the background. It was she and Dab who were alone together.

CHAPTER
2

Tree wouldn't have ever known Brother Rush was a ghost if there hadn't been a little room in the house. The little room was no bigger than a walk-in closet. They couldn't get a bunk bed in the room, it was so small. She and Dab had rooms with big double beds. They weren't great, large rooms but they were very comfortable. She would never call the closet room a *room*. You wouldn't want to show it to somebody as a *room*. It was more like the end of a room. Like an alcove made too small, with a folding door across it to hide the mistake.

Dab said once that the little room could be a walk-in closet. What did that mean? Tree didn't know; she had somehow missed that bit of knowledge. She couldn't get it that you could walk *inside* a closet to get your clothes out; then, you walked out of it again. It just didn't make any sense to her.

The walk-in closet-room was small. They stored stuff in it. They put what they didn't need there or the things they would someday have fixed.

"M'Vy be havin some extra time and we gone get that stuff fixed," Tree would say.

There was a wide, round table in the little room. It held all kinds of things—a broken television, pieces of things. Magazines from ages ago that no one had thrown away. Tree discovered coloring books that she had

18

colored in when she was quite a small child. Now when she had nothing to do, she would go in the room and have a relaxed look-see through some of the magazines. Six months might go by before M'Vy would think to buy new magazines. Then Tree would tell her to buy *Seventeen* and *Ebony*. From *Seventeen*, she found out how the best kind of girls were supposed to dress, act and think. She read *Ebony* because it had lots of pictures and she loved to see gorgeous-looking black folks doing well.

ᐟThe table was stacked with about everything you could think of. Magazines, dusty comic books. There was the television; part of a chair, its soiled canvas seat ripped. Half of a black telephone. A cardboard box of old, tired-out shoes. Tree would handle her old shoes one time and marvel at how small they'd become. Knowing they hadn't become small but that was always the way she thought about them in relation to herself. *They* had become small. A lot of junk stuff. And some nice, tiny football players from some toy game in wonderful poses of running and tackling; a few quarterbacks throwing, and a kicker kicking. Some of the players had their faces and hands painted white; some were painted black. They had belonged to Dab at one time, probably.

Who you belong to now? Tree wondered at them. She was fond of tiny them. Likely she had played with them, too. She felt she knew them, but she didn't remember.

One day she and Dab had a mind to clean off the big, round table in the little room. They did it one weekend, taking their time. It was done for her, so the table would be her play table and the room her playroom. She needed the private space better than her bedroom, different, because she had what was called a *ream* of white paper — more than four hundred separate sheets. And she liked to draw. She could draw two to six pictures a day using the paper from the ream. Now she could draw at the table.

19

She was careful of the amount of paper she used. Ream wouldn't last forever. Who knew when someone would remember to get her another? M'Vy got it somewhere. Who knew what Saturday Muh would come home and be in the right mood for Tree to ask for more paper. One of the pictures she drew was for herself, alone, and the rest for whoever had to see what she was up to in the room. She didn't talk about her drawings—who could she talk to about them? They weren't anything too special. Just people and houses and trees. Windows with curtains. Lots of space. Families.

She forgot most of the drawings as soon as she'd done them. The one for herself she dated and put her name at the top. Put it away in her room. Didn't even think about it. But she had a record of many months of pictures.

Sometimes Dab came in the little room. He would pull at his hair and his skin. He would be looking at everything in the house. When there was nothing left for him to see, he would come into the walk-in closet little room. He would look at it. This happened, too, when there were no girls in bed. Standing there looking all around at the stacks and stacks of junk, like he had lost something. Then he would actually feel the absence of something the way Tree did, as if the painful lack were a living, breathing force.

So it was the two of them had cleaned off the table for her. And that was why she had found out. The cleaned table. Brother Rush.

She came home from school. Dab came home and quietly went to his room; closed the door. Maybe he was by himself. Tree wasn't about to go knocking on his door to find out. She was home, safe; it was Friday. They said in school it was going to rain the whole weekend. It was raining outside now. She was wet. She felt tired, fagged out, with jumps of nerves up her arms and down the backs of her legs. Back muscles so tight and jittery.

Gone split myself down the middle, feel like, Tree thought. M'Vy, when!

She hung up her raincoat. She wore a sweater under it with blue jeans. Now she took off the sweater, put her books down on the floor and wiped them with the sweater.

The house was so quiet. She was in the foyer, which was narrow and dim. She hadn't bothered to turn on a light. She was bent over her books in her bra and jeans. She pressed the sweater on her books, and it absorbed most of the wet from her return-papers.

Good grades. One of her teachers wanted her to take tests for Black Achievement. Tree wasn't too sure about that. She had this conversation with her, Mrs. Noirrette, the English teacher. Black woman, at least sixty. From the Islands. Different, but nice.

"I'm telling you truth, deah, Teresah. Yah could be getting full scholarship monies for deh entire college program when you graduate. Yah have dat ability, chad. Now is deh time to begin taking tests, don't yah see. All what is needed is deh cone-fee-dahnse, deah, in yahself."

Tree had stared at the woman long and hard. Mrs. Cerise Noirrette. You couldn't tell about teachers.

Think they class, Tree thought. Then they dog you down.

She didn't know. Maybe she would start taking some tests. Usually she skipped school when they scheduled those all-day scholastic-average tests.

Who need 'em?

She thought about doing her homework. But if M'Vy didn't come on Saturday, she would have the whole weekend to face.

Save the homework, be safe, like most times, she thought.

She went to the little room to draw, to relax herself and

21

maybe fall asleep until either she or Dab got hungry and they decided to fix something; or she would hurry with Dab out into the rain for some fast food. There was a "Colonel" just a block or so on the avenue. She was getting low on cash. She had small bills hidden all over the house, case somebody break in.

Tree sometimes fell asleep on the floor. It was warm in the little room, like a hot box. It didn't have a radiator but it had steam pipes. The whole building had steam, which was unusual, Tree had heard. For her, the little room was about the most comfortable, private place in the whole house. If she ever got it cleaned out of stuff on the table and junk all around, she could put a sleeping bag in it and live in it. That's what she would do one time, if she and Dab ever found a way to get rid of the junk. They needed to pool their energy to do the hard, dusty work of it.

And paint the little room. Tree knew a paint color that was really tough. It was the palest, creamiest chocolate. And an antique white ceiling. Then she would have the room for good. Have the big, round table and a sleeping bag, and herself.

Maybe a small fridge, like they say in *Seventeen* some best girls had in their college dorms.

Not like her own bedroom. She knew about college, shoot. She knew nobody was gone give it to you, she didn't think. But she might take the tests. She'd have to see.

Feeling almost important from a teacher taking time with her. Standing out in the hall. Classes changing. Where everybody could see a busy teacher taking time with a special student.

It was Friday. Rain. Wind. Outside was dark and stormy.

Think nothin to it.

She came in the little room to peel away her worries. She came to draw.

She saw the strangest light. And Brother Rush. The way he had been in the street, although Tree hadn't seen him today on her way home.

It shocked her, seeing him.

Haven't seen you all week!

But she wasn't scared.

Dude! You beautiful!

There, dressed so fine, with one gloved hand up to his ear and the other supporting his elbow. His legs were crossed at the ankles. Dressed to kill.

She was about to say to him, What you *doin* in here— how you *get* in here! So full of happiness at seeing him again, so much she wanted to tell him, if she just could have a chance to talk to him. But without coming on to him first. She'd come on first if she had to, though. Yes, she would, too.

But then she saw. Saw and couldn't help seeing; couldn't keep herself from believing.

Brother was in the middle of the table. Not standing on the top of it in the middle, but *through* the middle. He was standing *in* . . .

In it? *In* it!

. . . *in* the table.

The door closed behind Tree. She leaned for it; then fell against it as it shut. Brother Rush was smack through the hard wood of the round table of the little room. She knew, all right.

Be a damned ghost.

CHAPTER
3

Tree stood for a long time. She heard the rain outside dripping from the top of the window frame onto the cement sill of the window. She heard cars sounding sleek, and the hollow rumble as they passed over manhole covers in the street. She couldn't tear her eyes from what had to be a ghost through the table.

Fear crawled up her legs. Cold flopped in her stomach like a dying fish. The fish froze solid, flaking scales of ice slivers that made her shiver violently. She was shaking so hard she thought the teeth would shake out of her mouth. She realized that the shaking and the cold were not the same things. The shaking was fear at what she was seeing. The cold came from the thing before her.

Say ghost brang cold, she thought fleetingly. How you know it be in the room.

Suddenly she noticed herself. Standing there the whole time in her bra. Pink and new, it covered her neatly; yet it was a bra, and she was modest.

"Wait I get my sweater," she told the ghost through the table. "Be right back." Murmuring through clenched teeth.

She got out of there fast. Her head felt like someone had filled it with air. It would float away. Only her neck held it in place. She found the sweater on top of her books in the foyer where she had left it. It smelled wet. It was a beige sweater, soggy and musty with the rain she had wiped from her books. She hurried on to her room then and clenched her jaw to keep it still. She threw the wet sweater in a corner and found a faded sweatshirt, a dull, pink color. Moving silently, she pulled on the shirt as she headed back to the little room. Tree didn't know whether Dab was listening to the sounds of the house. She hoped he wouldn't come out to see her and talk to her now.

And back again, standing against the door. No need to switch on a light. The little room had its own light. It was a dim light.

Came from what be a ghost.

Tree could see what she had to perfectly well. The table, and the good-looking dude through it. He was still there. Rush.

Tree had the vague notion that she had run out and come back again. She had done this so swiftly, with such a torment of nerves, she hardly realized she had left the room. She had been absolutely afraid; even so, she hadn't wanted the ghost to leave.

It was not so much the idea of a ghost that scared Tree. Not so much the word *ghost* and having to use it for the best-looking dude she had ever seen. Not what she pictured in her mind, floating down a staircase, or out in the fields floating. Not a nice cartoon of Casper Ghost on a Halloween. It was being there through the hard wood of the table, as solid as a rock. There, through the natural wood, with the hard wood in her mind, the ghost terrified her out of her mind. She would never have dreamed such a thing could happen in real life.

Brother Rush stood his ground. The hand that had been cupped around his ear now held something. It looked like an oval mirror, but it was not a mirror. What Rush held was an oval space shaped like a mirror, and it glinted at her. In it was a scene of life going on. Rush held the oval space wrapped in a sheet from her ream of paper, as if he thought he might cut himself on the space's edges if he didn't hold it in the paper.

Come from what I use to draw, she thought.

Rush stood there, not looking at her or anything else. Just looking.

Dreamy. You the sweetest dude ever I did see.

He looked as solid as she must look to him, if he'd been looking at her. He would have to know she was not a ghost—did he know that?

I know I'm not, the same as I know he be one, she thought.

Rush looked so real, he looked as if he'd been planted. It was then she wondered how she knew his name.

In the mind, she realized. Just there. Brother the prime name of his as Sweet be mine. Sweet Teresa.

There was a tired, old look in Brother Rush's eyes. Not oldness like a hundred-year-old man. But tiredness of a grown man of forty-five, like her neighbor, Mr. Simms, had.

Simms lost his wife and two sons in a car wreck all over the interstate. Simms hadn't been in the car. Just Bea, his wife, in the backseat with Gerald, asleep. Dennis, the other son, had been driving. And something had gone wrong. The mother probably never woke up before she went to heaven, was Tree's opinion.

Simms's eyes told everybody that nothing was ever going to get any better. He would never move any faster than he could move now. He would be no richer or poorer, he would not care more or less for anyone or anything than he cared at the moment Bea Simms crossed over into the realm of God.

That the kind of old be in Brother Rush's eyes, Tree thought.

26

She guessed Rush was nineteen or twenty. It would have pleased her if she could know he had just turned eighteen. She kept in mind to ask his age one time as she kept in mind that he was a ghost. He was still quite solid, though, still the one and only dude to her.

The sweatshirt she had on couldn't keep her warm. Yet she was aware of the moment when the cold turned into something she could live with. Fear was sealed inside her, like a tatter of paper from her ream. And if you opened the tatter, it would read: This is all the scared I can get.

Tree moved away from the door, closer to Rush. She lifted her hand to him and extended her arm. She had put herself in the way of Rush's gaze at nothing. Her arm was straight out to him — she was scared. Being sure not to touch him or the table. The space shaped like an oval mirror was right there almost in her hand. She could see her hand in it.

Thinking, if he be a ghost, that paper be one, too, and that space-mirror.

She saw her eyes in the space. She was looking down into the space and seeing herself. But it was not herself, not really.

Be a ghost in the mirror-place, she thought.

She was looking in and seeing herself walk away. She heard leaves crunch under her feet. Tree was in a place she did not know. It was so warm, and she could feel the water in the air. There was a road going off through open spaces. Warm and sunny out. Then, shade she could walk through. But if it was a hard-surfaced road, where did the sound of dry leaves come from?

Oh, I see, thought Tree, leaves at the side of the road. Is it fall?

Next she was in a house. She had a plump child in her arms. Tree didn't feel much like herself. For one thing,

27

she was too tall and she was plump, too, as though she'd had the baby-child maybe two years ago and hadn't taken off the weight.

That babe was so beautiful and was her second child. All she wanted to do all day long was ride with it in the porch *swang*, too. And she did, early in the morning. And even in the afternoon. The baby-child was a big doll. A girl, and wouldn't cry a lick as long as she held it.

Then Brother Rush had dropped by again. He had taken the baby-child and the first child, a boy, for a ride *much earlier*. And he had promised the baby girl he would be back.

The woman heard his car coming a mile and a half away, that's how quiet the day was out here in this country town. She just kept swinging on the *swang*, holding the clean baby girl. She had on a clean house dress of plaid—green and rust and yellow. The house dress smelled fresh and was comfortable. She hadn't made it. If you made dresses, they lasted longer. But none she made were so fresh or smelled so different as this one she had bought in the department store nine miles away. The Wrens' Department Store would put your purchase in a box with white tissue paper. And tie it up with a long piece of string.

As soon as she felt up to it and lost some weight, she would put a bonnet on the baby-girl and take her on a bus through Sunnyland with the new houses and all the white folks looking pleasant. And on through Housten and up on through Greenville Street into the city. And she would tell the child, Just look at all the cars! And the baby would laugh; she'd be eating ice cream. She and the baby would walk around and look for the Peanut Man.

This really tall man dressed up like a Planter's Peanut. She always stopped to pass the time of day with him. He would give her fresh roasted peanuts, maybe two teaspoons of them. If she wanted more, she would stroll around the corner; sometimes she would hold her big baby comfortably in her arms. Still in diapers—just those and rubber pants and the new pink bonnet. And go on in the Planter's Peanut store. Lord, it did smell good of peanuts in there! She'd buy a big bag, still hot, of peanuts with the shells on them. And eat them all the way back home on the bus. That baby-child would fall sound asleep smelling the new peanut smell. Ever after loving the smell of fresh, hot-roasted peanuts. And the baby-girl loved the smell of them the rest of her life, just as her mother did.

Tree was the woman, the baby-child's mother, and felt only a bit like her real self. She had no recollection of having had the baby. Yet she knew she had. Now she sat on the porch *swang*, bringing to mind that wondrous, fresh, hot-roasted-peanut smell.

And heard Brother's car coming on fast. It made the day shake down to utter stillness. Nothing moved or seemed to breathe as the car raced down Paxton Road at seventy-nine miles an hour. That was what Chin, her older brother across the road, used to say Rush was doing. The next thing she knew, Rush was parking in the driveway in a screech of his tires. He leaped out of the car and landed lightly on the grass. He stood in the shade a moment; then bounded up the steps. She smelled his Burma Shave as he sat down beside her and the baby in the *swang*.

She, smiling at him, and the child, holding out her arms to Brother the way she always did. Brother was the child's favorite daytime companion, as her father was her favorite evening one. The baby-child's father had a good, steady job. Rush, of course, had no ordinary work. He was the Numbers Man, known for his fast car and daring ways. He made out better than three men holding down steady jobs and all their money put together.

How I know this? thought Tree, seeing herself hidden

29

inside the woman. It was the last time Tree thought out-side of the oval mirror space for a while.

She was the woman with the baby. She was on a porch of a house she did not know and had never seen. She was having some fun, enjoying talking with this fellow whose name was Brother — Rush was his last name — who was the woman's brother, just as Chinnie and Challie and Willie had been.

Brother had the child bouncing on his knee. The wom-an went in the house and got her numbers. She had them ready for the neighborhood. Had them added up and the names of everybody and how much by each name and each number on a white sheet of paper. She had a good feeling today. She hoped for hits to make her commis-sion. She'd had a dream last night. All dark and weary dream, something flying. She woke up in a sweat. Even as she was waking up, she was hearing something flying through the dark. She'd stifled a scream for fear of wak-ing her good husband. But she did say to him the next day, Did you hear something in the night? And he said, No, nothing. She put a dollar on 823 and boxed it to trap it to her, to keep it from coming out in any form she hadn't covered.

Brother bounced the baby-girl. Tree-sa Belle, Tree-sa Belle, Brother called the baby, although that wasn't her true name. Her true name was Sweet Teresa Pratt after her own mother, Viola Sweet Rush Pratt.

Soon Brother had to leave.

Got my booking to do, he told the woman who was Vy Sweet and did not look at all like Sweet Tree.

Vy Sweet asked Brother to run a quick errand for her.

You'll make me late, he told her. But he could never turn her down. He did have to collect the numbers mon-ey and slips from all the runners, most of whom were his relatives. There was Binnie, his and Vy's sister. Binnie

30

was a runner and had the neighborhood next to Vy's. Binnie was always late getting her numbers route complete because of her dog, Ashland, Ken., named for Ashland, Kentucky. The dog had been run down by a car. He dragged his hind legs, poor dog, following Binnie around her route until the hair and skin of the hind legs rubbed off and the creature's hind quarters were raw, bleeding meat.

Got to go, Brother said again. He got up, kissed the baby-child.

Will you pick me up some books? asked Vy.

I got to hurry, said Brother.

But I don't got no books, Vy said.

The child began to cry. She raised plump arms to Brother. He lifted her up and spun her around, holding her under her arms, until she squealed with the delight of going in circles. Brother sat her on his head; held her there with his hands around her waist. She wrapped plump fingers around his thumbs and sat there, kicking her legs and rubbing her pink feet on his face. Brother swung her down into her mama's lap again. The child's face broke into little pieces. The biggest, grandest tears rolled down her face out of shiny eyes.

Got to go, Sweet, Brother told the baby. He was going, leaping from the porch and into the car. He blew the horn at the baby as he backed out. She stood up on her mama with a finger in her mouth. Big tears, falling. Vy Sweet had to laugh. Brother looked sad himself at having to leave the child. And her about to have a fit because Brother had to go.

Don't you upset your pretty self, Vy told her, and held her daughter close. She kissed her wet cheek. The baby-girl buried her face in her sweet mama's neck. And they glided back and forth and back and forth on the porch swang. And Vy dragged one sandaled foot along the floorboards and sang:

Oh, sinner man, you'd better repent!
Oh, sinner man, you'd better repent!
Oh, sinner man, you'd better repent!
Or God's goin' to get you on the judgment,
Oh, sinner man, you'd better repent!

She didn't know why she sang that particular song, except that she felt like it. It came from somewhere, out of some hot Sunday after a long sermon in church. She sang it until the baby, Sweet, had fallen asleep.

Gently Vy carried her into the house where all was dim, with window blinds drawn against the hot day. The child was growing, getting heavy. Vy held her close all the way up the stairs, feeling the warm breath on the side of her neck and feeling the soft baby face against her flesh. There was nothing on earth as dear as a fresh, sweet girl baby child.

Bless it! thought Vy. Thank thee for the worthy and good. Take that *boy* out of my life!

She thought of her firstborn, wretched son, her cross to bear through life. And as she climbed the stairs, she could hear the thump-thumping of that boy. She had to pass the room where she kept him on her way to put the baby to bed. She had tied him to one bedpost, had his hands wrapped good behind his back. He had deliberately got grass stains on his pants. And now if she allowed his hands free, he would pull down whatever he could get his hands on. All the perfumes and powders and lipsticks and combs and brushes—everything he could pull off the dresser and dressing table. After untying his ankles, he'd take everything out of the drawers and dump everything into the bathtub and run hot water over it.

The thump-thumping was the boy Dabney's foot opening and closing the closet door. He'd pry it open with his toes. Then he'd swing it shut with the flat of his foot and open it again with just his toes.

Vy stopped before the room where the boy was tied. The door was open. She saw him, licking under his nose where yellow snot hung in a glob. And swallowing it when he collected enough of the glob on his tongue.

Okay, okay, she told him, as softly as she knew how, still holding the Sweet baby by her neck and around her soft back. I ain't comin in there yet, she told him. But when I do, that be the last nose snot you ever eat!

After that, Tree separated from the woman. She felt she was looking down on the scene. All at once, she saw the baby girl, the woman, and the poor sad boy.

Vy had the baby down in her crib when she heard the front door open downstairs. She was sure it was Brother come back with new numbers books for her.

Carefully she placed the baby down and hurried to the top of the stairs.

Brother? Brother, I hear you. Just puttin the baby to bed. Be down in a fast minute.

She was whispering loud, hoping to goodness she wasn't waking the child.

A voice called back: No. No, Vy, it your cousin, Junior. It Junior, Vy.

Junior? Junior? she said, still remembering to keep her voice down. What could bring Junior off the job in the middle of the day? Junior? she called, more anxiously.

There was silence as Junior climbed the three steps to the landing. Vy was standing at the top of the stairs with her hands outstretched, touching the stairwell.

What? she said.

Vy, he said, his voice unsteady. He looked up the dark stairwell, searching her face.

She could see his expression plainly by the light from a small window on the landing.

Vy, there was an accident. An accident. It happen so fast. But he is killed. Vy, Brother be dead.

She couldn't hold on. Hands pressed on the walls simply gave way. She toppled over, like someone had pitched her headfirst down the stairs. Junior broke the fall with his body. But the impact of her dead weight knocked him backward from the landing down the three steps to the living-room floor. He was knocked unconscious when he hit the floor, but only for a moment. Vy had fainted, was like a rag doll sprawled across him.

Junior came to, hearing a tearing, crashing sound outside. He couldn't place the noise. Dazed, he moved Vy over and got up. Looked out, seeing the house on the corner. The front of it facing the street was covered with ivy. Always had been for as long as he could remember. But now the ivy was tearing loose and falling, crashing down with dirt and a few bricks to the ground. He stared at the extraordinary sight and felt shivers up his spine.

Brother be dead, he thought. The day the ivy fell.

CHAPTER

4

Without movement, without a sound, Tree came back. She found herself seated at the round table in the little room, with her elbows propped up on it. There was no ghost through the table now. She was sitting there, she didn't know how long a time. She felt she had come back from someplace, and then she remembered the place where she had been. It had been full of smells and sounds. Full of people she didn't know but who, nevertheless, seemed close to her, seemed familiar.

She heard a noise and gazed around the little room. She felt panic, for fear the ghost had returned. But quickly, she recognized the sound as Dab's feet shuffling toward the door. She hadn't noticed it was closed. But as Dab came nearer, she could see his lights. Yellow lights shining beneath the door.

He opened the door, came in in his shuffling shoes. "Do a little dance," he moaned. "Sing a little song." He did a little dance, grinning at her. She didn't smile; it was as if she'd forgotten how. She watched him bobbing his head. She leaned over to see the shoes with the little electric lights built into the toes. She and M'Vy had gotten the shoes for him in a novelty store. "Now you always be light on you feet," M'Vy had told him.

"Light on my feet," he said now. "See me, Sweet?"

"See you," she said, her voice coming husky, as though

35

she hadn't spoken for days. She cleared her throat. "What time it is?" she asked him.

He shuffled around the table close to her. A man's watch face was pinned to Dab's shirt. M'Vy had given him the broken watch. He'd taken the timepiece and put it through a pin and pinned it to him. Dab remembered to unpin the pin when he changed his clothes.

"Five thirty!" she said. "I been sittin here two hours. Ain't even started supper."

She didn't know where the time went. Dab took her hand, his eyes shining on her.

"Whyn't you tell me what time it is?" she said before she thought. He hung his head. His shuffling shoes shone brightly, but they did not move now.

"No, that's all right. It my fault," she told him. "Been sittin here like a fool. But Dab, guess where I been?" She looked into his eyes and she knew he wouldn't understand.

"Like a dream," she said. "Next time I go someplace, I'm gone take you with me." It didn't matter whether he understood every word she told him. Dab liked having her talk to him, to have sound between them.

"I figure, since you was there, too, then both of us can go there," she said. "Dab, it was so pretty there! It was country and a nice house and lots of people knew us."

Tree refused to put it all together. She knew that if she thought about it, she would maybe figure out more about the other place than she was ready to know. She knew the woman was Vy and the baby was herself, Teresa, and the boy whom she hadn't yet seen was Dabney. She knew what she had seen. But she had no more thought that it was true than anything inside a ghost place could be true.

"It's what it was," Tree said. "Right down inside a little oval space. It not possible, but it happened."

Dab wasn't listening to her. Sometimes he had bad days. On those days, he wore his shuffling light shoes. He was in his bathrobe, and she guessed he didn't have much of anything under it. His bare legs were ashy gray. He stood there, holding her hand, saying, "Owh-n, owh-n, owh-n." It was a monotonous one-note, almost a questioning that Tree could recognize even in her sleep, like a stray cat sounding miserable in the rain.

"Stop that, Dab," she told him.

"Uhn?" he said.

"You don't know you doing it," she said. She had an elbow still on the table, with her hand cupped under her chin. Sitting there looking at her brother, she had all the time in the world to know him and appreciate what little he was.

"You want to sit down? How long you been standing around?" Sometimes she needed to remind him to sit. He didn't always remember to sit somewhere and would keel over from exhaustion. Sometimes she forgot to remind him.

She saw that his legs seemed weak, and she pulled out the chair next to her and sat him down.

Dab sat down primly, holding his robe together. When he spent too much time alone, he would soon seem unable to take care of himself. Tree had to remember to play with him and pay attention to him every day or he would become younger and unable to do much. She had learned a considerable amount about taking care of an older brother who was unlike anyone she'd ever known.

"You hungry?" she asked him.

"I don't know," he said. He spoke in his careful, grown-up gentleman's voice.

She laughed with her hand over her mouth. "You don't know if you hungry," she said. "Dab, you can't tell, really? Think about your tummy-tum. It feel empty yet?"

She poked him in the stomach and smiled at him. When she felt low, if she could smile, soon she wouldn't feel so bad. "How you ole' stomach feelin, Dabney!" She laughed.

He thought about his stomach. He looked from her to his hand and put his hand over his abdomen. "Uh-huh?" he said. "Uh-huh? It hurt. It hurt me, Tree."

"No, it don't hurt you. You hungry is all. Right."

"Uh-huh," he said emphatically. "Got to eat."

"Okay," she said. She got a whiff of him. "Dab. Dab. Whyn't you take a bath?"

"Huh? Uh-unh?"

"Listen. I'll get some supper. Okay. While I do that, you get in the tub, okay?"

"Okay?" he said.

"You get in the tub, Dab. Do it. Now."

They got up. Tree went in the kitchen. She watched Dab go down the hall. He looked back at her before he closed the bathroom door behind him.

Tree went about finding food. There was meat, but no frozen vegetables. She stood before the open refrigerator, her hand poised in mid-air, reaching for the meat. She saw she was holding her hand exactly the way she had held it when she'd reached for the oval space in the little room, when she had gone away, she knew not where she had gone.

Who will bring more food?

She wondered for the first time whether M'Vy would come back before all the food was gone.

She always has. How come I'm scared she won't now?

Tree took out some hamburger. I'll have to make spaghetti sauce, she thought. Hamburger too frozen for patties.

Tree listened. She could be doing something, anything, but always a piece of her mind was attached to the welfare of Dab. She heard no water running.

"Dab?" she called, dropping the meat on the kitchen table. She hurried down the hall to the bathroom. "Hey, Dab." Knocking on the door. "Whyn't some water running?" She eased the door open. He wasn't there. Then she saw him lying in the bathtub. No water, just lying there on his back in his bathrobe, his hands behind his head.

"Oh, Dab, get on up from there."

He got up.

I did tell him to get in the tub, she thought. "Now, get out of the tub, Dab. I'm gone run your water." Obediently he got out of the tub and stood at her side.

She had the water running and made sure it was not too hot for him by taking his hand and letting the water flow over his wrist. "Not too hot?" she asked. "Not burnin you?"

"Not too hot," finally he said.

"Okay. Now. You get in the tub and take a bath. No! You take the robe off first, after I go out. You get in the water without no clothes on. What the matter you today, Dab? What going on in your brain? You know how to take a bath. You ain't no baby. You pretty smart, most the time."

"Owh-n't feel so good," he told her.

"What the matter, then?" she asked him.

"Owh-n't know nothin," he said. He made crying sounds, although no tears came into his eyes.

"Now come on." She took his hand again. "Everything okay. I'm here with you. You got to take your bath."

"Okay," he said. "But say that man he get out of my room."

Tree felt herself go still inside. She felt her heart sink.

"Wh-what?" She stood staring at him, "Wh-what you saying?"

"Owh-n't like him in there," Dab said.

She was pulling him by the arm, pulling him out of the bathroom and down the hall, until they were on the other side of the kitchen where they had bedrooms across from one another. She burst into Dab's room, knowing if she paused for a moment, she would never have the nerve to do it. She didn't think once about a robber. She thought only of Rush.

"Not a soul," she said almost calmly when she had slammed open the door to find the room empty. "What man you talkin bout, Dab?" she asked him.

"Be a man," he told her. "Can't lay down in the bed. Be a man in it. Right chere."

"Okay," she said. "You got to take a bath. No man now. If he ever come back, you tell me, hear? You tell me real quick. Just come find me. We gone stick close these days, you and me, you hear? Maybe M'Vy coming soon. Hope so."

"Me, too," Dab said. He became more like himself on a good day. "The water runnin still in my bath," he told her.

"Oooh!" she cried. "Almost forgot. Come on." She rushed him back. She told him again what he must do. She turned off the water and made sure he had two towels.

"Don't get no towel in the water. Use this yellow washcloth and this soap. You soap yourself good. Then you rinch off. After you rinch, you let all the soapy water out. You turn on water a little way until you got it just warm enough. Can you do that?"

"I can do it, Tree," he said. "Thanks."

"You feeling better now, ain't you?" she said.

"Yeah, I want my bath now."

"Okay. I'm gonna leave. You get in and be careful."

She left him. "Did you take your robe off?" she called through the door.

"Yeah, I did," came the softly muffled reply.

"I know you did," she said to herself. "I know you did," she called.

Went back to the kitchen, took the wrapper off the hamburger and tossed the frozen meat chunk in a skillet. She poured in some oil and set the skillet on the burner at medium low. She took an onion out, a can of broken mushroom stems and some dried parsley.

Got everything! Got it all.

And found more spices.

Oregano mostly gone, but it will do. Remind M'Vy we need some more.

Easily, minute by minute, she made delicious spaghetti sauce, using a can of Italian whole tomatoes and two cans of tomato sauce. She slowly added ingredients to the steadily thawing meat. Only after all the sauce ingredients had been put together did she remember to look for spaghetti. She looked everywhere, but there wasn't any.

How'd I let that get away from me? Well, there's potatoes or macaroni. We put the sauce on our baked potatoes.

She washed two potatoes. She went back to the cupboard for two more, for she was starved.

Know Dab gone be hungry. Dab! She reminded herself. Tree! You got to always have him on your *mind*, else something bad could happen. She quickly dried her hands and headed for the bathroom just as Dab opened the door and came out. He had a bath towel tied at his waist like a sarong. The bathrobe was folded neatly in his arms.

"Put my robe ina washing machine?" he asked her.

"Sure!" she said. "You lookin all clean, Dabney."

41

"I am clean," he said. "What you think I took a bath for?"

She laughed, amazed as always, the way he could seem to recover his mind from something as simple as a bath or walking out in the rain. Dab might stumble in to wash his face and come out of the bathroom again with an expression of alert quiet, which hadn't been on his face when he went in.

Dab walked through the kitchen, and Tree patted him on the back as he passed by. He looked like her big brother now.

"Proud of you, Dab," she told him.

"Ever-thang gone be okay," he told her. Dab always said, "Ever-thang gone be okay," something he learned some time ago and couldn't let go of. Other sayings of his he had had to practice long and hard so he could keep them in mind. Most of them had to do with his shucking and jiving with girls. Like, "You a pretty girl. Smart. No business bein out in the street. Ought to get back in school. I'll take you back. I'll stick with you." That had taken him a month of Sundays. And he had to take his time with the words or he would get them mixed up.

Once Tree had heard him get it all mixed up. She'd been leaning out of the window of the apartment. Dab and some girl were downstairs, standing by the stoop. She could hear them just as plain as if she'd been right there on the sidewalk with them.

The girl was giggling and trying to pull away from Dab, but not trying too hard. Dab was all slicked down and dressed sharp, like some hustler working fine and not going to high school. Too old for high school. That was the impression the girl had. He was being so serious with her, with an earnest look on his face. But he got it mixed up, saying, "You be pretty smart. No business bein in school. Ought to get out back in the street . . . take you, I will stick back with you."

42

He knew he had it wrong. His hand tightened on the girl for fear she would split on him, leave him with nothing but his mixed-up words.

The next thing Tree knew, he was shaking the girl by the shoulders, hard, while still trying to get the words right. He had them hopelessly wrong. Tree had to get down there and stop him. She would have to turn everything off on the stove first before she left, fearing fire. Things downstairs might take too long. She feared a fire in their apartment worse than anything. There were plenty of fires each week. And a cold, furious hate of fire stayed with her deep in the hollows of her mind. When there was a fire, people close by in the street looked at Dab funny. But Tree knew better. Whoever set the fires were not kind and gentle like her Dab. She knew. She could protect him by always being with him when they were home.

What am I gettin so upset about? Why remember the bad things like that girl that was scared of Dab in the street? Tree thought now. I took care of her, dint I? What I say! Yeah, but I got bad with her, and that wrong. What you gone do? Callin him a loony tune.

"Ain't no loony tune, neither," she had told that dumb girl.

"Yeah, he is," said the girl. "He your brother? He a loony tune, ought to keep him offen the street, hittin on innocent girls, too."

"Now look who you!" Tree had told her. She roughed the girl some and had to use some bad language, something she would rarely do. "An if I ever hear you say loony tune about my brother again, I'll make your nose never be the same—you know what I'm talkin about, too." And she would have. Would have taken her wide-toothed Fro pick like a weapon and raked it across that tender piece of skin under the nose between the nostrils. And would have stood there as that girl fell to her knees, helpless. There was no defense against the lightning pain of a comb raking.

What I'm standing here for like a dummy?

Tree was at the stove, her wooden spoon poised above the bubbling spaghetti sauce. The sauce had splashed on the wall behind the stove and all around on the white surface of the stove.

"Shoot!" she said and turned down the stove. "Look what it done!" she cried as Dab came up behind her to peer over her shoulder.

"Sure do smell good," he said.

"But look what it done! Gimme a sponge from the sink, Dab." He got it for her and she cleaned things up, sending him back once to rinse the sponge and squeeze the water out. Tree took back the sponge and cleaned up the streaks. Dab watched and put the sponge away when she finished.

"How I look?" he asked her.

She turned around. He had on clean wrinkled pants and a clean wrinkled shirt.

"I dint iron those clothes yet, Dab," she told him.

His face fell. "They lookin fine," she said quickly. "Just put some socks on your feet and you be fine."

He did as he was told; came back and sat down at the table.

She wouldn't ask him to set the table. It would have been too much to ask him to take a bath and set the table all on the same night. She set the table herself, tossing the plates in place expertly. Napkins, silverware and glasses were placed. When all was ready, she sat at the head of the table and Dab sat next to her on her right. Always she sat at the head of the table when M'Vy was away, which was so much of the time, Tree was reluctant to move when Vy did return.

Tree brought the spaghetti sauce to the table in a flowered bowl. She put a potato on Dab's plate. He waited

44

patiently for her to open the potato. He delighted in see-ing her take the fork and make diagonal marks across the skin. She would then push in at each end and the white, steamy, cooked potato would puff out. It made Dab laugh every time.

"See?" she told him and buttered the potato, seasoned it with salt and pepper.

They ate. They drank Hi-C. There was Mountain Dew to drink but Tree felt Hi-C was more nourishing. It was grape Hi-C.

Quietly they ate. Tree would have liked to have a can-dle burning on the table while they ate. There were can-dles in the cupboard. She didn't feel like going to the trouble of getting one.

She watched Dab trying to eat his food.

"What wrong with your hand? Why you holding on the fork like that?" she said.

He had the fork turned over. Had it pressed on the fatty part between the thumb and index finger.

"Dab, you cain't eat that way. Turn the fork over." She turned it for him and put it in his hand properly. His hand was limp-feeling, hardly any strength in it. She held his left hand a moment, and it wasn't any better. "Make a fist with your right hand," she told him.

"Uhn," Dab said. His hands fell away. He flopped them around, and his fork splattered the spaghetti sauce on his plate.

Tree fed him without a word about it. "You sure actin funny," she said. He grunted or *uhn-uhned* at her. She ate and she fed him.

Dab, darn! Carefully she scrutinized him, all that she could see of him from the waist up. His skin was ashen. Dab failed to use skin cream regularly. He wasn't some basketball player. Tree knew the basketball players and how sensitive they were about their skin.

Think they some babies. Too pretty!

They rubbed themselves with Vaseline Intensive Care clear to their crotches until their dark legs shone in a high ebony sheen.

Ball player sayin to a bench warmer: "Whyn't you white baws ever get ashy?"

The white boy wait a long beat to answer. Finally, "We get ashy, only it don't show on us."

Tree smiled to herself, remembering. She had a soft place inside for all basketball boys. Grimly she studied her brother.

He chewed and chewed.

Like that potato some kind of hard bone, she thought. He lookin peaked this evening. Darn! All I need.

CHAPTER
5

When the doorbell rang its fuzzy, soft buzzing, Tree was up as bright as sunrise.

"M'Vy!" she yelled and ran out of her room, pulling bedclothes with her. She banged on Dab's door with her fist. "It's M'Vy!"

She ran to the door and quickly unlocked the spring locks and the police lock, without once remembering that M'Vy had her own set of keys to the door. She must have been still asleep. She had been so positive. It could have been a robber there. It might have been any stranger ringing the doorbell first thing in the morning. How many times had M'Vy warned her always to take her time and think?

Tree pulled open the door. There stood the old lady who helped out cleaning up the place every Saturday morning. Miss Ole Lady Cenithia Pricherd. Tree had forgotten about her, forgotten about the list she'd made of chores for Cenithia to do.

"You wanta call the mess Miss Pricherd make and the time she waste makin it some cleanin?" Tree had told M'Vy one time. "Dab can do better," Tree had said. "All she do is drank up the half 'n' half in her coffee and eat up the danish."

M'Vy had scolded Tree for speaking ill of the less fortunate. She told Tree that Miss Pricherd had nobody in the world to take care of her. The woman was sixty-seven years old and hadn't ought to be working, M'Vy had said.

"Shoot," Tree had told her, "I know some sixty-seven-year-old womens that actin thirty-five and gettin away with it, too. But Miss Pricherd find a warm place to eat and rest, all right. An act to you like she doin some work. Only I'm here to see what she do and it me be doin most the work."

"Tree, you suppose to help out Miss Pricherd," M'Vy had said, "cause I can't pay her hardly nothin."

Tree had felt herself ready to break down and cry. Her eyes filled with tears. M'Vy saw this and told her, "Next time I'm to home on Saturday, I'll have a talk with Ceni-thia. Tree, you know I trust you, Heart."

Heart was what Vy called Tree when she wanted Tree to know how much she depended on her. Tree knew she shouldn't have spoken so harshly about Miss Pricherd, and for a long time, she had felt ashamed of herself.

Things went along. Miss Pricherd still didn't do much. She had ways of not working that got to Tree. Tree wouldn't have minded so much if Miss Pricherd had simply said she had to sit down every half-hour for ten minutes, instead of her hiding in the kitchen and sneaking the food out of the refrigerator. So the old woman was hungry; Tree could understand that. She didn't mind giving food. But she couldn't stomach the idea of somebody sneaking around and stealing.

All this going through her head as she stood there holding the door open and blocking Miss Pricherd's way. Disappointment formed a lump in her throat that it was not M'Vy.

"You gone let me in or what?" Miss Pricherd said.

"Oh, I'm sorry," Tree said. "Good mornin, Miss Pricherd. Come on in. M'Vy didn't make it yet."

"Huh," was all Miss Pricherd had to say.

48

Tree had hit on a plan to make Miss Pricherd get a certain amount of work done before she paid her. She always paid her at five o'clock every Saturday afternoon.

"M'Vy make you a list this time," Tree told the old woman once she got out of her bundles of shapeless clothes down to her working housedress and sat down in the living room to rest.

Tree hurried to get the list she and not M'Vy had made.

Okay, she got to rest. It all right, let her rest, Tree thought. She controlled her indignation. I know how long she wait for a bus and transfer. I know she got to walk from there to here. But I get so mad at her, I can't help it!

Before Miss Pricherd could say anything about the list Tree handed her, Tree said, "You sure tired the first thang in the morning." Saying it as sweetly as she knew how.

She watched as Miss Pricherd slowly read the sheet that Tree had carefully written to represent M'Vy's handwriting. She an old woman, Tree thought, but she don't have to wear glasses to read. How old is old? Maybe she not old. Maybe sixties is just beginning old. Forget this ole lady. Don't you let her get to you and Dab.

Miss Pricherd eyed Tree up and down when she finished reading the list. Tree didn't dare look smart or anything. You couldn't talk back to a church woman who was part old who had come to clean. But you could look strong, Tree thought. And so she did. She stood there; she was getting taller, too, growing a little bit every day. She stood as straight as she could in her blue nightgown. Had on her three-quarter-length blue velour robe which she had got for Christmas as a complete surprise from M'Vy.

49

M'Vy the only one in the world to give me presents; give Dab presents, too, Tree thought.

It came to her all of a sudden: If M'Vy get runned down by the bus, if there be some mugger, nobody to brang us nothin! Where are the relations?

The relatives were dead, what ones M'Vy had. Tree knew it. There had been three brothers way older than M'Vy and all three of them dead and gone. And a sister, dead from strokes. Where are the kids? Wouldn't there be some little kids grown up now? Why come me and Dab never hear nothin about them. And the ghost! Who the ghost?

The few hours of having M'Vy with them on her short weekends at home were precious. They would let M'Vy give them all she had to give, and they let her talk about what she cared to talk about. Tree and Dab never had time to find out about the past; they had so little of the present.

Tree sighed, holding on tightly inside herself. Don't know what it is with me today, she thought. Maybe wake up too quick with that doorbell buzzing.

This, within the time it took for Miss Pricherd to give her deathly cold looks up and down after she read the list a few times.

"Vy never did give me no list before," she said. "Who need a list for this bitty place, huh? Been cleanin houses since I ten years old. And never need no list for nothing."

With the tips of her fingers, Miss Pricherd placed the list on the seat next to her. It lay still and white, a paper from Tree's ream.

"I'll help you wit it," Tree said, "once I get Dab up and get him dressed and he and me have some breakfast."

Miss Pricherd snorted at that.

She sound just like a cow, too, Tree thought.

Her serene expression never changed. "We better get started," Tree said. She stood up and waited. She wasn't going to leave Miss Ole Lady alone for a minute, not in the living room and sitting down.

Miss Pricherd sat, smiling to herself. Her eyes seemed covered with a gray film this morning. Her face held little light. There was an unkind smile across her mouth. It pulled her lips to the side in a bitter smirk. She wore her hair straightened in an old-fashioned page boy with bangs. It was shoulder length and jet black. It was blue black.

Fake and phony, Tree thought. Wonder if it's a wig marked down.

"Ought to put you brother where they puts people lak him," the woman said. "Shouldn't be somebody lak you in charge of some retarded."

Tree didn't know whether this last was meant as a compliment. But there began a slow burn inside her.

"Dab is not . . . is not . . ." She couldn't say the word.

Miss Pricherd laughed soundlessly. She had teeth that were gray or brown. They were crooked, with spaces in between them. There weren't a lot of them. "You know that boy ain't got good sense," she said. "He gone rape somebody, then they put him where he belong."

Tree felt burning hate like she never knew she had for anyone. Her fists clenched and her lips trembled so, she couldn't make a sound. Her eyes filled with tears; but then she got hold of herself. She began gulping air as if she'd been running. Miss Pricherd looked alarmed. Still mean, but not quite as certain that she had everything in hand. She had her arms straight at her sides; hands, knuckles under, pushed at the couch. She didn't get up but sat there, alert to Tree's next move.

"You have the list to do like M'Vy say before this day

51

be over." Tree's voice was steady and dead cold. "M'Vy say not be paying for nothing not be done."

Tree turned away, ready to get the day started. Then she turned back. "Don't be cuttin on my brother. I'll hurt anybody, on account of Dab being so good and kind."

"Nobody cuttin on him, shoot," Miss Pricherd said. Slowly, painfully, she got to her feet. "Whew, Lord!" spoken softly, as though she meant it. A look of pain swam across her face to drown in the black of her eyes. It was not fake.

Tree left her and turned her thoughts to her brother. "Dab," she called, coming to his room. She knocked lightly on his closed door. "Dab, son," she joked. "You get on up outta there. It wasn't M'Vy. Be Miss Pritcherd come to clean."

Dab would have been up long since when she first said it was M'Vy ringing the doorbell. Why hadn't he gotten up?

She pushed open the door. "Dab," she said.

He was lying in bed on his back. She came up close and leaned over. He was lying there staring at the ceiling. His arms were outstretched on either side. Tears rolled down his cheeks.

"Dab! Dab! What a matter wit you, Dab?"

"I can't move," he said.

"What you mean, you can't move? Come on, Dab. We have to get started cause maybe M'Vy come on in later and want to take us shopping."

"I can't move," he said in a whisper, and his eyes closed on his tears.

"Dab, what you *mean*, you can't!"

"I mean . . . it hurt so bad when I do."

"Where it hurt?" she demanded. "Show me and we can look it up in the doctor book—what it called—the *Merck*. Any pain at all, it'll tell us what to be done."

"It not . . . one place," Dab told her. "I move, it hurt me everywhere. Lying on the bed . . . it hurt me."

"But where it hurt you?" She almost yelled at him. "It got to hurt some*where*."

"All over. Don't turn no light on. It hurt my eyesight, too."

"Oh, Dab," she said. "That don't make no kind . . ." She stopped herself, recalling that Miss Pricherd had said Dab had no sense. His tears convinced her there was something very wrong with him. Dab might make crying sounds every day. But tears fell only when he was in real pain.

"I'll get the heating pad," she told him. "Dab, you cold?"

"No'm," he said.

"I got to touch your forehead, see for sure."

"Cain't stand no touching, Tree," he whispered, fighting back the tears.

She pressed her knee on the bed, leaning over him. Dab hollered out in pain. She jumped back, staring at him in wonder.

Don't make no kind of sense, she thought. How can it hurt him when I just touch the bed? Where do it hurt him?

"You lie and don't move, you hear? I'll brang the heating pad." She didn't know what else to do. "I'll fix some breakfast for you," she said.

"Give me some time," he whispered. "It be gone after while."

"You mean you had it before?"

"Sometime. Come in the night. Gone by morning."

"Whyn't you tell me, Dab?"

"Be gone after while." He was panting with the effort of talking. His face looked pale and clammy.

I got to reach M'Vy! thought Tree. "You just rest then, okay?" she told him. "I'll be back."

53

She left him, closing the door again behind her. Outside in the hall, she listened for Ole Lady Pricherd. Heard her in the bathroom, running water in the sink.

Tree searched for the heating pad in the hall closet and found it by feel in the dark. There was no light in the closet. She went back to Dab, and it took her minutes to get the pad on him without him hollering out. It hurt him, she could tell, as she placed it on his chest. But he seemed to want it.

"You use it when it be hurtin you all over before?" she asked him. He said yes in a tired whisper.

Carefully she plugged it in behind the bed. She put the dial on Medium High and waited to see if Dab could stand so much heat. Soon he breathed deeply in and out. The pad went up and down on his chest in a steady motion.

"Dab?" she said softly. He was dozing, but he could still hear her. "You musta been up all night wit it," she said resentfully, upset that he had not called her for help.

"Dab?"

"Huh?" he answered.

"Does it hurt you with the pad on like that?"

"Huh?"

She would have repeated the question, but she realized he had fallen back in the mind, was the way she thought of it. His mind was somehow less now, she felt.

"It don't hurt so much now, do it?" she said.

"Uh . . . unh," he grunted.

Maybe the pain makes him think better, she decided. And the pain leave him and he cain't think again.

"You can doze," she told him. "I'll fix you something. What you think you wantin?"

It took him a minute to answer. She saw his lips part, and so she waited. "Make . . . something go down . . . down easy."

"Some mush?" she said. She knew how to make good, yellow cornmeal mush.

"Yeah," he said.

"Some toast wit it?" she said, not worrying a minute about the way she spoke — how M'Vy told her she ought to pronounce words as correctly as she could.

"Nah'm," Dab said. "Just milk mush."

"All right," she said. "Take me a minute."

She went to the kitchen. Dumb Lady Pricherd had finished in the bathroom. Tree didn't bother to check it. She would check everything later when Miss Pricherd was at the end of the work and doing the kitchen.

Probably only sweep the dust up in a damp rag stead of washing the whole darn floor, too. Know her kind.

Miss Pricherd was now in Tree's bedroom, running the vacuum. That was something. That was what the list said for her to do. Tree fixed the mush, taking her time. She realized Dab probably needed sleep more than he needed food. She melted a 600 Stress Tab multivitamin with zinc and iron and a 1000-unit vitamin C in the mush. They were almost out of the Cs. She would have to remind M'Vy to replace them.

M'Vy!

Tree put the lid on the mush, leaving the wooden spoon in, and turned the burner off. She went to the telephone. On the wall beside it were important phone numbers. Emergency numbers for police and firemen. The ambulance number and the Crisis number because she wasn't sure but she thought Dab did get hold of some pot sometimes. And all the numbers where M'Vy ever worked with the names of the women of the houses. Tree called the last number and nobody answered so she figured, if M'Vy was working there, she must be out marketing. Tree made a star beside the number to remind herself to call back. She called the next-to-last

hite lady answered, said she never heard of
Made Tree so mad, she hung up on her. How
say that when M'Vy had worked there for
time? Just mean, was all, or simpleminded. Tree
called a few more numbers but got nowhere. She called
the last number again; let it ring fifteen times, but there
was nothing.

She hung up and went back to fix Dab his breakfast.
Put the steaming mush in a bowl on a tray with a cup of
half 'n' half and sugar and took it in to him, with the
spoon sticking straight up in it, it was that thick. Good
mush.

She stood there beside his bed pouring the milk, just
enough so it wouldn't cool down the mush, and added
enough sugar to satisfy Dab's sweet tooth. It only took
her a moment. Eyes closed, Dab had one arm flung up
over the pillow. He breathed easily, relaxed.

"You better, you?" she said. "I got mush right here.
Smell it?"

"Uuum-huum," he murmured.

"Well open your eyes! Can you sit up now, Dab?"

He thought about that a second. She could see his body
grow still. "Too afraid to try," he said thickly.

"Try," she urged him. "If you can move your arm up
like that—did it hurt to move it?"

"Huum?" He turned his head, looking up, only then
realizing he'd moved his arm. He brought it down slowly
to his side. He winced once, but that was all. "Better," he
murmured. "Much, much better." He sounded intelli-
gent again.

"Now," she said, "ease yourself on up the pillow.
Don't strain yourself. Do it easy."

Dab pushed with his feet until he was sliding, pushing
the pillow up against the headboard, until he was half-
sitting. Opened his eyes. They looked clear. He reached

for the tray. Tree placed it on his lap as lightly as she could, in small stages. She did not let go of it until she was sure the pressure of it wouldn't hurt him.

"It okay," he told her. "Just my legs and my back ache now."

"I'm sorry," she said. "We gone have to see about that." If I can't reach M'Vy, what do I do with him, she wondered.

She thought about the only other adult she could turn to. Not her! But if I have to, I will.

She went out, headed for her bedroom, satisfied that Dab could feed himself. She found her room cleaned, the bed made. Smelled Pledge furniture polish.

Didn't tell her to change the sheets, she thought. But she ought to know.

Lifting the bedspread, she found clean sheets under a clean pillow.

Good! Wouldn't be nice, have to sleep on some dirty ones another week. Never could put on sheets too good. Pullin them corners on clear tight.

Tree went to the living room and found it hadn't been straightened from the night before. There wasn't a huge mess, but it needed dusting and vacuuming so it would smell fresh, like her bedroom.

What she do, go work in the kitchen so she can eat? Tree rushed out but then slowed down so as to walk normally and not act like a spying child. When she got to the kitchen, Miss Ole Lady Pricherd hadn't been there. The mush had got hard and caked on the sides of the saucepan where she had poured it out. Everything was just as Tree had left it. She looked around her. All of a sudden she went still, hearing a sound. In an instant, she was racing from the kitchen. And bumped her hip on the edge of the table, she had been in such a hurry. She fell low with the shooting pain of it and limped along. It took her time to straighten again. She was by the living room, in the hall, with tears smarting her eyes.

"No!" she whispered, hurrying as best she could.

No!

It was the hall through which she and Dab left and entered the house each day. At the far end of the hall was the little room, the walk-in closet of a room that was hers to play in. It was hers.

Mine!

Standing there, clutching the doorknob of the closed door to the little room, was Cenithia Pricherd. In the other hand, she had Tree's instructions for cleaning the house. She had heard Tree coming, seen her limp into the hall. She was poised now, in exaggerated concentration, studying the list.

"Uhn-uhn," Miss Pricherd said. "Nothing bout this room on the list. This room I always dust, even if it be for only some storage. Uhn-uhn. Now why it not on this list!"

She stared at Tree. "Girl, what chew got in there?"

Tree crept toward her, shaking her head.

"Maybe you brother keep some stolen goods in here. Got something tough goin, too. Yo'w alone so much, wouldn't put nothing past you. See your mama, tell her, too. Yo'w got it made! What you got in here!"

"Miss Pricherd, no!" Tree shouted. At that moment, she knew why she'd been saying no, why she'd left the little room off her cleaning list. She reached for Miss Pricherd's hand, too late. Ole Lady turned the doorknob and had the door wide open.

Junk of the house piled around the floor. Tree's round table was clear. Dead set through the middle of it was the dude like no other. In a wild beating of Tree's heart, the terrible, cold miracle of him appeared before her eyes in the pose he always took. He did not look at them. He stared outward or inward, who could know? He was dressed in his silky, dark finery, one hand cupped to his ear.

Cenithia Pricherd whinnied like a horse. "Y-ow!" she hollered, in agony. "Y-ow-ow! Y-ow-ow!" and fell to the floor in a clump of trembling bones.

Tree bent over her, holding her by the shoulders, while Brother Rush stood his wooden ground. He was visible for three or four seconds more. Then he faded in a waning of mystical light.

Tree tried lifting Miss Pricherd but fell to her knees herself. Who could have imagined that Brother Rush would come again so soon? Something began to rise in Tree. It came, hard and loud, bubbling through her lips. She stared at Ole Lady Pricherd out cold. Her shoulders shook. She threw back her head. And laughed.

"Oh. Oh!" she laughed. "Whew! Keyed up. Oh. Oh." She couldn't stop herself.

That picture. Miss Pricherd seeing him through the table.

It did not occur to her to be surprised that Miss Pricherd could see Brother Rush.

Man, I could've sold tickets! Whew!

Calming herself, she placed a hand on Miss Pricherd, who seemed to stir.

"Miss Pricherd? Miss Pricherd?"

Bet you be careful about every closed door from now on. Hee! Fear you gone see something. How you gone open the bathroom door or a closet door? Oh!

Tree giggled herself free of the pain that had been in her hip. It was not long before Miss Pricherd came to her senses. And for the next hour, Tree had her work cut out for her. The first thing she had to do was keep Miss Pricherd from fainting away every five minutes at the thought of the ghost. She accomplished this by some smooth talking and by fixing the Ole Lady a complete breakfast. Bacon and orange juice, an egg omelet, which was a Tree specialty. At the end of the day, Tree fed her enough coffee ice cream to get her good and mellow. Nothing to it.

CHAPTER
6

There seemed to be night in Tree's house. Even when it was day, often she would have to turn on the lamps. Dab was in bed in this late afternoon and the false night within the apartment. He was lazing more than he was sleeping.

"Nothing hurt so much that I cain't turn myself over," he told Tree. His long fingers touched his face, probing as though to see if it were broken.

Miss Pricherd had finally got herself together and gone home. She admitted she hadn't had anything to eat since the night before. No supper of any kind. No evening snack or anything.

"That why you seeing things," Tree convinced her. "I'd be seeing stuff, too, if and when that be my case."

She had Ole Lady Pricherd believing that what she had seen through the table in the little room was merely shadows playing tricks with her eyesight. That she was weak and feeling faint from the lack of nourishing food. Tree even led her back to the little room so she could see for herself there was nothing there.

"Got to be sure," Miss Pricherd whispered, coming on reluctantly behind Tree.

Tree prayed Rush wasn't in there, a ghost through the table.

Just stay away till she out of the house! Lay low! Tree

begged in her thoughts. Dude, I know you come back here to see me. To take me *out* again.

She entered the room and there was nothing ghostly anywhere. No feeling of cold and no mystery of haunting light.

"See?" she showed Miss Pricherd.

"But it was the most real thang I ever had come over me, too," said Miss Pricherd. "Never gone let mysel get so short, I don't eat for that long again. Uhn-uh."

"Well, I'll pay you today everything you owed," Tree told her. "But first you must get this here room done, please." She knew how to sound polite.

"Stay while I clean it," Miss Pricherd ordered.

Tree stayed, sitting sideways on the windowsill, watching the outdoors and lifting her feet when Miss Pricherd went by with the vacuum.

"Bet somebody give yo'w good money for this mess," she told Tree as she dusted off the junk stacked all around.

Tree didn't take up the conversation. She glanced hard at Miss Pricherd to see if she might be thinking about swiping some things from the little room.

Wouldn't do that if I was you, Tree thought. Never can tell *what* be watching you!

She smothered a smile in her hand. Best not get too friendly with Miss Ole Lady, she thought. Maybe Brother want her to see him just to keep her straight. Oh, I wish I coulda told her. But she never would recover. Probably all this time, believer in ghosts. Believer in a Holy Spirit. And never seen *nothing* but scared she might. I coulda said it was the Holy Spirit but what she gone do about it? Make this place some miracle shrine. Shoot. Let her think it was hunger. And hope Brother don't come back while she here.

Miss Pricherd finished up the house better than she

ever had. Tree made sure to give her plenty coffee ice cream, which was Dab's favorite kind, right after she'd done the little room and before she started on the living room. After eating the ice cream, Miss Pricherd had been almost nice. But she eyed Tree every moment she could whenever Tree was in her vicinity.

Thinking maybe I'm a soft touch, Tree thought. Thinking about getting what she can but she not so certain. When she through, I'll give her an apple to take home, plus the money she made today.

She gave Miss Pricherd the apple in a lunch sack, paid her and let her out of the house. Telling her good-bye and being slightly standoffish. Tree locked all the locks again. It was five o'clock, she realized suddenly, and time to get another supper ready.

Where do the day go. Where *did* it go, she corrected herself, for M'Vy said she must talk and think the English language properly.

M'Vy didn't come home after five, or six o'clock, either. But by six o'clock, Brother Rush was back.

Tree checked the little room exactly one hour after she let Miss Pricherd out of the house. Going down the silent night hall with its ceiling light on.

She stood at the closed door, paused with her hand on the brass doorknob. She had been drawn irresistibly to the room but she could not at once bring herself to turn the knob. In the movies, people looked through keyholes. But this door had only a button beside the knob inside. Push the button and the door was locked. By turning the knob again, the lock was released. Now the button was broken inside and the door never would lock.

How come nothin ever get fixed get broken in this house, Tree wondered. And thought of Dab. Who gone fix him?

She made sure he had everything he might need

throughout the day. She helped him up and into the bathroom two times.

What will happen if sometime I cain't get him up in time, she wondered.

Today she had got him up. He was only aching, he told her. Inside herself was a scared place, anxious, where lay coiled her troubled thoughts about the sickness he had, whatever it was.

She heard no sound on the other side of the door. "Nothing to stop you," she told herself. "He ain't hurt you or anybody else."

She opened the door on a peculiar light. It brought her a sudden, crushing sadness. And next there was Rush, big as life. Tree sucked in her breath. So good-looking in those same sharp clothes! She knew fear — how could she help not knowing it? Still, she was overjoyed to see him.

She whispered at him through the table, "I'm so glad to see you, Brother. *My* brother be sick, too."

That suddenly, she had thought again of Dab. Rush made no response standing there. He held his pose, one hand up to his ear. The other hand had that one sign, that space. A shining space, as if it were an outline of an oval, shining with daylight. If she went closer, Tree knew she would go through the space. She knew Rush had come to take her out.

"If I should go, what's to become of Dab?" she said to Rush. She saw him as clearly as she saw anyone. But now she knew something she had not before taken time to think about.

"You a dead man," she said out loud. "Be how they pose some dead in them old-timey pictures I see once before M'Vy saw me looking and taken them away. Some grown-ups posed and lots of dead babies. Babies holding bottles and Teddy bears just the way they would when they alive. One man lyin in the coffin reading the news-paper. Somethin! Say he wanted to be the first man to die that way, but he didn't make it. Paper say somebody else die before his dying time. Did they pose you standing up with your hand to your ear?" She heard her voice stop.

He did not speak. He stayed through the table.

"Wait. I know what."

She left the little room and went quietly to Dab's room. "Dab, see if you can get yourself up again. Come on with me a minute. I got to show you something."

"Huh?" he said. Gently Tree took hold of him, direct-ing him out of the bed. "I'm just lying down," he said sweetly. "Be suppertime?"

"Comin soon," she said. "But come on to the little room with me. There's somebody there. No kind of rob-ber, though, so don't you be fraid. You ever seen a ghost?"

Dab smiled broadly and nodded at her, but she could tell he didn't understand what she meant.

"Hurt you to walk, Dab?" she asked. Carefully she led him across the room and through the door into the hall-way.

"My side hurt all the way up and down," he told her.

"Which side?"

"Right side, all the way up to the back of my head, and then down the back of my knee and my right foot, too."

"That sure be something funny," she said. She had kept him going down the hall. Now they were at the end where the door was closed to the little room.

"It won't hurt you," she told him. "Dab, it want to take me out and I want you to come, too."

"You got a date to go out on?" Dab said. She didn't answer. She opened the door. There was a peculiar light.

Rush hadn't changed a bit. He held the bright, shining space. Around the edges of the space, they saw greenery waving in the breeze. Smelled summer blossoms.

Dab was fascinated. Tree knew he would be. Nothing standing still ever scared him. But moving figures confused his mind. On television, life moved too fast for Dab, so rarely did he watch it. Yet he could concentrate on anything standing still. Why he loved statues in the park, Tree knew, and pictures on the walls at the museum. He would put his face so close to museum pictures that the guards would come up to him and tell him to move back. "Dab, you tryin to get inside the pictures," laughing, Tree had once told him. And he answered, "Yeah! Yeah!"

Tree knew all about what Dab wished for when he concentrated on things that would not move. Once, two years ago, M'Vy had some time and thought it a good idea for them to see a museum and, after, an amusement park. They went to the museum first. Dab liked it. He hated the amusement park, where everything swirled and glittered, moving around and around and never holding still. He up-chucked his hot dog and ice cream and put M'Vy in a bad mood.

So when Dab saw him through the table, he said, "Yeah? Yeah?" softly.

"Be Brother Rush," said Tree. "He cain't hear you or see you, I'm guessin, cause be a ghost," she told Dab. "You ever seen a ghost?"

"Uh-huh?" Dab said, his voice rising. "Un-huh?" he said again.

"When! When you see some ghost!"

Dab didn't answer. He was concentrating on Rush there before him. He was seeing how Rush had one hand cupped around his ear. His other hand held a space of green and sunlight. Dab looked on the space opening held so still. Breathed the scent of fruit blossoms.

He pointed at the space. He moaned, shaking his head.

"Don't you want to come see it?" Tree said. "I know it scary, but come on, anyhow."

She put her arm around him and took his hand, steering him forward. Dab pulled back. Suddenly he stiffened and stood at attention.

"What a matter you, Dab?" she said. She peered into his face. "You gettin sick again?"

But he wasn't sick. She sucked in her breath. Dab's mind was gone. "So that how it look!" she whispered. She realized that, unlike her, he need not go close to the space in order to get there. He was gone, his mind somehow entering Rush's green and sunlight by his concentration from where he was. He didn't have to reach.

Maybe when a mind was as simple as Dab's, going to unheard-of places was easy.

She let go of Dab's hand and hurried to see into the sunlight. She reached for it through the greenery. "Where'd you go?" she said, and then, "Don't you hurt my brother!" Spoken to Rush, or whatever it was that could in some way transport them and might harm them. "Oh, you scare me!" she cried.

It felt as if her arm had gone within the space clear to her shoulder. The space was right before her eyes. She heard summer birds and felt warm breezes.

"Why you doin this? Why you doin this?" Softly she spoke.

It felt like her nose and forehead, her cheeks and mouth, slid through sunlight. They were on a road, going fast, going up. She felt clammy heat wet her hands where they creased and folded. She had on white, soft underpants. Nothing else. Warm wind gave her goose bumps on her moist chest and shoulders. She was standing on her pink sun dress where it lay crumpled at her feet.

She scrambled down on her knees on the woman's lap.

The car pulled hard up the road. She could hear it, Ga-ruhin, Ga-ruhin, hurting her ears. She could feel the warm sunshine on her arms out the car window. The woman's hand held her around her middle. Wind was on her face on top of the sunshine. Wind took her breath away.

Slow down, Brother, the woman warned. They took a sharp turn, squealing up.

Her plump hands covered her nose as the wind swept across her face on the sunlight. She breathed through her fingers, trapping the sunlight. Gently the woman pulled her back in through the open car window. She fought and fought until she once again had her elbows out of the window. Her head, shoulders and chest were outside. The woman sighed and held her strongly, both hands firm around her belly.

Tree was the child; she was also the woman. Yet she knew she was still Tree. The awareness of herself would leave her, she knew, as it had the last time she was drawn into this place. For now, she was child, was woman. She was Tree, observing.

You gone turn us over, too! the woman yelled. She was sounding scared.

Baby sis, how'm I gone pull these hills if I slow down?

I can't look! said the woman.

I brought you and them kids up here to see the sight from up high. You can see Wilberforce and Jamestown. See fifty mile on a clear day like this. Almost to the Ohio River.

You kiddin! The woman was startled by that. Clear to Cincinnati? From up here? Brother, you a lie!

You look hard enough and you see a glint and that be the city reflecting in the Ohio River.

Well, I have to see that, the woman said.

What I'm sayin, Brother said.

The little girl saw how high. It was silence and green shining light as far as she could see. The car had stopped, and there was stillness. She sucked her fingers, thought about the light. Now she felt hot; her cheeks were burning.

A commotion began in the car. She pulled herself back in from the window. She knew what the trouble was. Turned around, sat down on the woman as the small boy came tumbling over the top of the seat from the back, where the woman had put him. He came, headfirst, to see better. He was upside down between the man and the woman, trying to get himself turned around. He couldn't flip over, so he kicked his legs. Tree was there, seeing, but felt herself fading. She was the woman, her gorge rising. She was the girl child, seeing pictures, shapes. She became frightened as the woman holding her stiffened and let go one reassuring hand.

The woman bent down and came up with a stick. She struck the boy's legs back and forth, whipping, back and forth. The boy's scream rang out. She, the girl, saw his thin legs in short pants tremble and kick. His legs were up the front seat where his head should have been. She was forced to see his toes curl as they were struck and struck. She watched his legs stiffen like boards.

The man, Brother, tried to get the stick out of the woman's hands. All this in silence, as sunlight of the high place filled the car. The two of them struggled.

Don't hit him anymore, said Brother. One of these days you gone hurt him bad, too.

You saw him, said the woman. You saw what he did, trying to provoke me.

He was only tryin to get in front with his baby sister. He just wanted to see everything in front. You know how he loves to hold the wheel.

Brother had the woman's wrists, and the stick trembled the same way the boy's legs had. They struggled; all at once, her body went limp. The child sitting on her lap felt it. She was ready to cry as the struggle went on and on and the small boy stayed upside down. Now she whimpered and sucked her fingers. She wanted Brother to hold her but the woman held her tightly, with an arm around her middle

The woman gave in. Brother took the switch and tossed it into the backseat. The child heard it land softly. The small boy was still upside down. Gently Brother righted him and put him on his lap behind the wheel. The boy liked that. He had his back to her and the woman. He leaned the side of his face on Brother's chest and felt for the wheel. He found the wheel with his skinny fingers and held onto it, caressing it without looking at it. He loved all things that did not move quickly. He loved the wheel when it was still. He loved Brother, when Brother was still, like now. He loved statues and quiet.

Brother took his handkerchief from his breast pocket and wetted it from a mason jar of white liquid he kept under his seat. He touched the boy's legs with the wet handkerchief where welts had risen. They looked like red worms wrapped around his legs. The boy winced and stiffened at the touch.

Shhh. Shhh, Brother said. It'll hurt only a minute. Then it'll cool you and it won't hurt again.

Brother folded the handkerchief and put it under the seat with the Mason jar of liquid. He took up the Mason jar again as an afterthought and took a quick drink from it. Then he tightened the lid and put the jar back under the seat.

The girl watched all this. Tree was gone. Dab was gone, if he had ever been there. In the car now was the woman, Brother, the girl and the boy. Brother ran his hand along the boy's shoulder as the boy rested against his chest. He didn't look at the boy or the woman. He was looking at the scene out of the window. The woman stared straight ahead. The child was standing, looking out the window. Her face was against the woman's; her fingers were in her mouth. She moved her fingers so far down her throat that she gagged. The woman slapped her hand away from her mouth. She whimpered and cried for a moment; but then thought better of it. All was still in the car.

Until Brother started the motor and they were rolling backward.

Be careful! said the woman. You just at the edge.

There's ten feet before we at the edge, Brother told her. Why you so scared of high places?

High places ain't it, she said. It's you, reckless.

Not me. I just know how to have some fun, he said.

He still held the boy on his lap. The boy didn't know where to put his hands as noise came up from beneath his feet. Brother placed his hands on the wheel next to his own.

You got to help me now, Brother said to the boy. Do what I do.

The boy looked grave. He let his head loll back against Brother. Brother had to hold his hands to keep them on the wheel. The boy looked down, away from the windows, to avoid seeing movement. If he looked outside, he would become sick all over himself and his favorite uncle. The feel of the wheel moving under his hands frightened him.

They breezed down and down. The little girl was half out the window again.

You ever see a child like this one? the woman said admiringly. Behind stickin up all sassy!

Better not let her lean out too far, Brother said. Tree branches so close sometimes on these narra roads.

Tree. That who she be growing to. Tall. Tree, the woman said.

On and on, in sunlight and shade, until the road was

71

monotonous. The girl fell asleep, face on her arms resting on the window frame. She awoke as they entered the town, drenched in the fragrance of wild roses. All the older, smaller houses and bushes and vines of flowers ranging in color from white to deep purple. To her, the bushes were sweet-smelling circles whose scent could not be separated from their shape. The very sight of them made her dizzy and took her breath.

They turned in the gravel driveway of a familiar house, with a porch and swing. The car shut off and the doors opened. She was holding onto the door, trying to keep everybody in the car. She stood, stamping her feet on the woman's lap. But the car had too many doors; she couldn't keep everyone in. The Sunday drive was over. She thought of crying, she was so sad that the car had stopped. But she saw Ashland, Ken., and he made her laugh.

Ashland, Ken., guarded Binnie, the woman's sister, who sat on the porch swang. Binnie's husband, Lee, was sound asleep beside her. Ashland, Ken., belong to Binnie; and he was spotted orange and brown, and crippled.

She watched the dog open his mouth, grinning at her. She lunged for him, for any part of him she could get her hands on and squeeze with love. But Ashland, Ken., dragged himself away to Binnie.

Sweet, now don't you pester him, Binnie's shrill, nervous voice commanded. Binnie raised her cane.

That stopped her, and she stood there on the top step with her fingers in her mouth. Watching the black cane. The sleeping Lee, leaning to one side. Aunt Binnie.

Look what the cat drug in, said the woman. She eased up on the porch with the little girl at her side.

Hi-Hi! yelled Binnie. Her voice cut a harsh track through their senses. Binnie pulled at her shriveled, paralyzed arm. It drew tightly to her chest. She pulled it down. Her cane clattered to the floor as she momentarily forgot where she had placed it. The little girl lunged for it. The dog dragged himself; then hurled himself at the child, growling and baring his teeth.

The woman screamed. Instantly Lee was awake. He lurched for the dog, caught Ashland, Ken., by his collar, and pulled him away from the child before he could bite her.

Binnie, you got to put that dog away! said the woman. She grabbed the child, swinging her up protectively to her chest. Soon the girl was sitting on the woman's hip, riding sidesaddle. She was not at all frightened, just watchful.

Dog will do about anything to protect Binnie, said Lee in his slow, easy voice. He went on as if nothing had happened. How you doin, Vy? How you, Brother?

Fine, said Vy. How you doin?

I'm fine. Brother added, how you doin, Binnie? spoken kind, with respect for the profound mystery of illness.

Binnie's return greeting curled out of her mouth in a gurgling of nerves. She was sweet and kind, Brother knew, but as high-strung as a lead guitar. She was a good numbers woman and played her book with one quarter of the gambling women in town. Vy played with another quarter. Vy's husband, Kenneth, played with the men who were poker players. Easy enough to get poker players into numbers. But Binnie would have to quit. He would have to see that she quit. How long could they go on, watching her teeter down roads, a pathetic, crippled soul with her crippled dog dragging behind her?

The girl saw the boy come out from his hiding place behind a tree and climb the steps to the porch. He gathered silence around him, did not look at anyone. He opened the screen door to go inside the house, and the woman did not notice him. As long as the little girl rode on the woman's hip, the woman would forget the boy for hours at a time.

Brother saw him, though, and reached for him, holding the boy against his legs and prying his hand from the door. Where you goin? Brother said. Come sit on my knee. Come on, don't go off by youself like that all the time.

The boy lowered his head and kicked backward against Brother's shin. Brother had to step away. A frown crossed his face. He let the boy go. The boy went inside.

The girl wiggled down off the woman's hip. The woman wanted to sit down, so Lee got up to give her room.

Whew! she sighed, fanning herself. That baby gets heavier every day.

She no baby no more, Lee said. What you expect? She a growing child.

Uh-huh? said the woman. An she love to ride. We did ride! Brother about to run us overtop the hills. Fixin to . . . She clamped her mouth shut suddenly. Her eyes ran to one side of her face, then the other.

The girl turned to the door and managed to pull it open. She stepped up high, following her brother. Her brother was not in sight inside the living room. She knew exactly where he had gone. And she followed. As she climbed up the stairs, she could hear her Uncle Lee chuckling on the porch.

Cute as a button, he said. Gone be pretty when she grows big. Have to tie her in, too.

She liked the stairs. She could hold onto the banister and watch her feet. She loved the feel of the carpet under her toes. It was red and soft. She watched her feet all the way up, with both hands holding onto the banister so she wouldn't fall. The woman had shown her how to hold on.

She could hear them outside on the porch through the open windows.

Woman, you crazy, Brother was saying. You got a husband better than anybody. And you gone leave him? So what if Ken do spend some money? The man make it, don't he?

It was nice being almost up the stairs and the woman was not holding her, gripping her close and making her hot.

Up the stairs, there was an open room where they kept the toys the man bought them. Big, stuffed toys for her and trains for the boy. She asked for trains, too, but never got them. The boy let her have his. He loved stuffed animals that did not move.

She knew exactly where to go. Into the front bedroom. It was dark but had a small window of light. The boy stood, facing her. He leaned against the side of the bed.

She knew where to find the rope. Knew where the woman hid it. She went in the closet and found the rope in a shoe box. She asked the boy, You want me tie you to the post? I can do it. I can be the woman, see? She lifted the rope toward him. He swatted it out of her hand to the floor. His mouth turned down. His eyes filled with tears. Eyes wet and shining at her. The boy climbed up on the bed and covered his head with a pillow.

He cried and he cried.

She walked in the closet, put the rope away. She never lifted it again.

CHAPTER
7

Tree had no recollection of time's passage. She found herself in the kitchen with Dab, and she had not noticed any movement or change of place. The two of them must have made their way from the little room, down the hall and into the kitchen in some kind of dream.

The girl going up the stairs, maybe that was coming in here, Tree thought.

Her mind felt blank, and she had the sensation that she was evaporating in the silence. But then, suddenly, she was completely herself. She stood up and began doing what had to be done. She turned on the kitchen light. There was no ghost of Rush to be seen or felt. And there was no other place that was also another time and beyond her understanding.

You think too hard about it and you'll go off your mind.

She went about preparing the supper. It was six thirty.

"Should've had it all done by six o'clock," she said, not to Dab particularly. Dab was lost in himself. She talked to feel less anxious.

"Nothing to make but some macaroni and cheese. Dab? That be okay?"

"Un-huh?" he said, quietly. "Un-huh."

"Dab, come on back. It over. I won't take you there no more wit me if you don't stop it," she warned.

"Uhh?"

"Dab!"

"Wha—?" he said. "Wha—?"

"Listen, don't say everything twice like that, hear? It sound funny, like you not all there. You all right, Dab?" She stopped what she had been doing to look him over.

"Feel sick to my stomach," he said.

"That was probably because of the car ride," she said. She was still, silent. "But how could that be? Dab? Did . . . did it seem like there was a car ride? And you come over the top of the seat and she . . ."

"Didn't go in no car," he said. "Went to funerals."

"What? *Funerals?*"

"Yeah, Uncle Willie's funeral."

"Uncle Willie?" she said, hardly breathing. She felt her heart skipping. "I never even met Uncle Willie. He did die, I think I remember M'Vy say, long time ago!"

"Yeah? Yeah?" Dab said. He swayed in the chair. His face was ashen. "Don't take me no funerals no more."

"Oh, Dab!" Tree kneeled down beside him. "I didn't know. Oh, that's scary! I thought you was wit me!" She hugged him. He kept his hands resting in his lap. He had his knees together. Bony knees, with tremors through them. He was weak, barely able to lift his hands. "Come on, I'll help you to bed," she said. "Bring you some food in when I get it ready."

"It all right," he said. "I want stay in here wif you."

"Dab, *wit* you. I mean, *with* you. You know what M'Vy saying about stuff like *wif*. But you can stay in here wit me if you want to. You just don't think about anything. Funerals! I went in the car. You were there, in the backseat. Don't worry," she said, "I won't take you back there again, lest I can't help it."

She began preparing the food. She knew how to make macaroni and cheese from scratch.

"No package noodles for us, is it, Dab?" she said, needing to hear the sound of her voice in the still apartment. "Talk to me, Dabney," she said playfully. But he didn't feel up to it, she could tell. Some days Dab could say whole sentences. He would talk for ten minutes straight. It had been some time since he'd been that good or had felt that well.

Tree knew how to make white sauce. She grated cheese and put a cup of it with chopped onion in the sauce when it was ready, while the noodles boiled.

"Key to everything is get it all done at the same time," she said. "M'Vy say it is the art of cooking, timing all of it to the split minute."

In the middle of mixing cheese sauce with cooked noodles in the carefully greased glass bowl, she thought to ask Dab something. "You say funerals, plural? Who else be dying?"

"Unh? Huh?" said Dab. "Nothin. Nothin."

"Dab, don't say things twice."

He made crying sounds, so she quit trying to get his mind clear.

Must've been Ken, my daddy, she thought. M'Vy say he die all a sudden. Heart, after Willie die. I don't remember him.

"It's all right," she told Dab. "You in here with me, and we good people." She smiled at the proper sound of her words.

She made bread crumbs out of toast, first letting the toast cool to get it hard. She sprinkled the crumb-and-cheese mixture on the macaroni-and-cheese dish. She shook paprika over the topping and placed dabs of margarine here and there.

"See, Dab? Did I do a good job? See?"

"Yeah-uh-huh. Uh-huh," he said.

She felt sad for him, for his lonesome self inside the small amount of mind he seemed to have. How had it happened, she wondered, that he was born with trouble in his brain? Or did it happen later?

She put the dish in the oven and turned the temperature to 350 degrees. Finished, she washed up the dirty dishes. Standing at the sink, fear commenced crawling up her neck. There had been no warning. She stood, frozen, her hands in the soapy water.

Somebody come in here behind me—am I losin my mind?

She didn't dare call out to Dab and make him fearful. Any time she sensed danger and Dab was nearby, he would feel the danger from her. That was why she usually remained calm about everything.

She wiped her hands and got up her nerve. She turned around, looking at everything as she turned. Sink, counter, chopping board. Refrigerator. Hot-water heater over in the corner. Stove. There. Dab at the table. Nothing through the table. All was as it should have been. She walked over and calmly turned the oven up to 375 degrees.

That what it should be in the first place. I made a mistake.

"Come on, Dab," she said. She took his hand and pulled him up. "We got to wait for the food. Let's go read some."

She led him into the living room. She kept her eyes on her feet so she wouldn't have to see down the hall to the little room. She wouldn't give that room a second thought, wouldn't shape the words to say it in her mind. That was how she got them quickly into the living room. Dab stretched out on the couch. She sat in the easy chair right next to the couch and propped her feet up on the coffee table.

"Now," she began. "What you want me to read?" She

79

had already taken up the book. No matter how many books M'Vy provided them with when she had the dollars for a paper cover, Dab only wanted the same one.

"Read it. Read it," he said. " 'The Time I Got Lost.' "

"Now that ain't the *book*," she told him, sweetly. "That just be a chapter." Showing off her education and what she knew about books. Dab loved for her to play like that, as though she were his private teacher and teaching no one else, ever.

"Now," she said. "The name of the book is—" She waited for him.

It took him a minute. She knew it was hard for him to focus his mind. First he would have to think: paper cover. book. pages. book. what it called. what it called. title! no. no. name, then title. She imagined that was the way he came to know.

"Got the man's name on top," Dab said. "Big name in black. Warren Miller. Yeah. Yeah. Then, brown. Boy, sittin by garbage cans. Two cans. Boy with tennis shoes. He sittin on air."

"No, Dab, look," she said. "He sittin on the curb. But the drawing don't show the curb cause you already know he got to be sittin on something, if he sittin there by the garbage, and he is. So why paint the curb in? See, that's how the artist think about it."

"So why put some garbage cans there?" Dab said. "So why you got to have the boy sittin at all?"

She laughed and laughed the way she always did when Dab said that. She could remember the first time he said it. M'Vy had been reading to them and she had laughed and laughed. Now she felt just like M'Vy, shaking all over and laughing. Saying, "You ain't dumb, you ain't that dumb!" And laughing some more.

"You want me to tell the title?" he asked.

"Yeah," Tree said, calming down again. "Tell the title and we can get started."

"Title is . . . *The Cool World*, born, 1959."

Tree laughed and couldn't stop. "No, oh, God. Dab, not *born!* They copyright it. See, it say 'Copyright, c., 1959, by Warren Miller.'"

"M'Vy say it bout the same," he mumbled. "Don't laugh so hard, Tree."

"I ain't laughin at you, Dab. I'm laughin wit chew, believe me."

"I ain't laughin. You see me laughin?"

"Okay, then, I'm sorry," she said. "I won't do it again. Didn't mean nothin by it." He was silent. "Okay?" she said.

"Yeah? Yeah?" he said. Like a crazy, she thought, and kicked herself hard inside for thinking so mean.

When Tree started, she made her voice low and clear so Dab would have an easy time losing himself in the loving words.

The Cool World was about certain dudes living before she and Dab were born. They were street dudes in a gang. The gang was the Royal Crocodiles, and the enemy's gang was the Wolves. Dab liked the part that didn't have anything to do with the gangs, although he liked the whole book because it told about the Street, and Dab loved to think he was cool as some street dudes. But he wasn't cool.

Put Dab on the Street for one day and night, and Tree knew he would be dead or, worse, a junkie, or a slave, stealing for somebody, by the next morning.

"Now," Tree began, "here I go. You be quiet now, Dab. Ready. Chapter. 'The Time I Got Lost.'" She read, going into the words as though she had been born in them. Dab went with her. He loved the true words of "The Time I Got Lost."

"'Whut I remember is I remember the red dust an how hot it get from the sun on it,'" Tree read. "'An I uset to go bare foot and the dust would ooze up between

81

my bare toes like mud. That whut I remember earliest when my Mother lef me down home with Gramma Custis & I was 3-4 year old I guess.

" 'They uset to get up real early in the morning down there like 5 oclock and we eat breakfast with Grampa Custis before he go down the road to work for Mister John Snipe. Or Snead or Snade. Somethin like that. Snead I think it was. He a farmer and Grampa Custis work the farm for him. On Sundays Grampa Custis get all dress up in a black suit an we all go walkin to that beat up church where he preach.'

"You want me to skip to the part about some eggs?" Tree asked Dab.

"Yeah. Yeah? Skip on to there," Dab said.

"So here it is," she said, and started again.

" 'Sometimes we have an egg on the grits an after I thru eatin I uset to go out to the side of the road an watch the 7-8 year old kids walken to school. Some of them wearen shoes. One day I follow behin them to the school house. Half the windows broken an I can hear them singin My Country Tisuv Thee. Then I walk back home thru the woods cause I afraid of meetin Mister Snead an his dogs and I got lost. I got lost in the ferny woods . . .' "

"Ferny woods! Ferny woods, yeah!" yelled Dab.

"Now quiet down or I cain't read you," gently Tree told him.

He quieted, and she continued.

" 'I got lost in the ferny woods,' " she started the last sentence again, " 'wanderin aroun an finely I just set down near a little pond an just wait till they come for me. I remember how hungry I was. I just set there on a log an waited an sang church songs.

" 'Grampa finely found me. He laugh when he see me sittin there. He say. "Boy you got the most worrying Gramma in Snade County. Praise GOD I foun you for if not I never go home again to Mamie." Then he pick me up an carry me out of the woods to the road. I guess I was maybe a block from the road all the time.

" 'Goin down the road Grampa singen a song about the LORD and I can hear it vibratin in his chest an his heart goin boom boom boom.' "

"Boom-boom-boom!" Dab said, raising his head to look at Tree. "Boom!"

"Okay," Tree said. "You want me skip some."

"Uh-huh? Uh-huh?" Dab said. "Skip to tippin his hat."

"Okay," Tree said. "Now, shhh, so's I can." Dab stayed quiet, laying his head down, and she started again.

" 'He (Grampa) tippen his hat to all the white men an sayin. "How you Mister Snipe. How you Mister Snout. How you Mister Snups." ' "

Dab laughed and laughed, and Tree had to wait for him; then she went on.

" 'They all smile at him an say like "Hows the preachin goin Revrent?" an like that. Same people that kill him after I leave to come up North with my Mother.

" 'One man say. "That you boy Revrent? He the spittin image of you. You doin all right for an old man.' " Tree skipped one line that she didn't like, then read, " ' "Yessir. Thats right," Grampa say. "Yessir."

" 'That time he foun me lost in the woods he carry me home an when Gramma seen us comin she come runnin down the road to us. Cryin. An took me an carry me the rest of the way.' "

"End of chapter, 'The Time I Got Lost.' " Tree closed the book. She slid down in the chair. She didn't look at anything in particular. Dab was lying still, easy in himself. They sat, not a word between them, minute upon minute.

83

Dab finally spoke. "Say what it mean, Tree." He always had to ask before Tree would tell the meaning.

"Well, see, the boy, Richard, who come down from the North and go back there, is telling this story about his grandpaw. But that ain't all it, just the story," she said. "It what goes on there when Richard get lost. He know to wait. Cause he know the grandpaw gone come find him. How he know. Because. Love is it. That boy stay put in the ferny wood because his lovin Grandpaw goin to get him if he wait and wait; that grandpaw is gone come. And he comes, too."

"Yeah? Yeah?" Dab said.

"Yeah, and it don't matter what the Man do or say to you, the Grandpaw and Grandmaw got all the love inna world for the boy. Grandpaw Custis just yessir the Man to death, it don't matter a-tall because they keeping the boy, Richard, close. Then the enemies gone and kill the Grandpaw for nothin."

"Uh-huh-uh-hun," Dab said, quiet and low. There was sadness coming over him, making him twitch.

"But they can't kill the love in the boy," Tree told him. "The love the Grandpaw leave him, that was what the old man willed him. The boy never, never forget."

The two of them were so quiet in the house, they knew exactly what sounds there were in the apartment and what sounds belonged to the street. Others, to the city. They knew how to be together. And they were peaceful, knowing for certain why the chapter "The Time I Got Lost," from the book *The Cool World* by Warren Miller, made them feel so close. They had the will. They could wait out the time.

Later, Tree went into the kitchen to see about the macaroni. It was bubbling. She turned off the oven. She made salad of cabbage and carrots, with mayonnaise to hold it together. She set the table and poured two glasses of grape Hi-C.

"Yeah," she said, smelling the good smell of macaroni. It was eight o'clock now. She'd nearly finished this day of work and of taking care of things.

"Sunday comin," she said softly to herself. "Maybe then I can sleep late."

CHAPTER
8

Tree woke up in the middle of the night. She opened her eyes on the dark of her room. There was a line of light, like a thin pole the length of her door. It was light coming in from the hallway. Her bedroom door was open a few inches.

Hear somebody if they try to walk in. What you do if somebody come? Is that it? she thought. What wake me all a sudden? Somebody come creepin in the hallway? Fear was a cold shape under the sheet with her, making chills down her spine.

That's okay. I got my protection.

She was afraid. But silently she slid her arm off the bed and down to the floor. Right by the post of the bed, she kept a slender cylinder of tear gas. All you had to do was press where there was an indentation at the top. She knew using the gas could help her, if and when she had to use it on someone. It would give her time to get away and wake up Dab.

What Dab gone do? Maybe just let him sleep. Get myself out and down the fire stairs and call the law. Be better and quicker. But they say the law never respond if you a woman calling. Think it be a man beating you. Why you call.

The tear-gas tube did the best thing for Tree without her ever having to use it. It made her feel safe when she woke up so alone at night.

What had awakened her this time? It was always some little thing. Was Brother Rush in the table? A ghost wasn't something little.

Ow'nt care. Not going to get up and see.

Maybe she had heard Dab holler out. Dab often hollered out in his sleep. Tree would wake up every time. His mystery of pain had come back, and it maybe worried her into light sleeping. After supper, Dab had got sick and vomited his food.

"That's a shame," Tree told him, "all that good food." When he felt better, she tried to get him to eat the macaroni again but he wouldn't.

"How about some salad?' she said, but he wouldn't have it.

So she made him some grits of yellow mush with hot milk. He ate about half a bowl. It didn't stay down. She helped him change his pajamas that smelled sour from the vomit. And worried how she would get him to bathe in the next few days if he stayed so weak and sick.

How to handle him if I cain't touch him, she thought. Only now did she understand her predicament.

She had put Dab to bed. He'd been in considerable pain. Asked her not to turn on the light, which, he said, hurt him all over.

How can that be, she wondered. Light don't have pressure. Do it? No, cain't feel nothing of it. Unless you have a bad headache. Then light be hurting you in the eyes and make the headache worse. Maybe it like that for Dab all over him.

Tree lay in bed, feeling cozy. Slowly she brought the teargas tube in her hand under the covers with her.

Suddenly she knew why she had awakened. She jumped out of bed. Stooped, placing the tear gas next to the bedpost. Smothering a cry of astonishment, she hurried into her velour, three-quarter robe.

Swear, I'm a loony! Half-asleep until just right now!

She fought the robe and couldn't find the armholes in the dark. Struggling, she was determined to look neat by the time she left the room.

What Tree had heard: the sound, clink-a-*chunk*, in the living room. Her bedroom opened on the hallway to the living room. She had heard clink-a-*chunk* clearly in her sleep. She remembered. She must have forgotten as soon as she was half-awake. So familiar a sound, it made her want to cry. She knew she would cry. Already there was a lump in her throat.

Struggling into the robe, precious blue, she tied it tight around her and tiptoed out of the bedroom. Once she was in the living room, the hall light lit it well enough without her turning on a lamp.

There was the big pocketbook. It was black suede. The pocketbook rested on four gold knobs. The fabric would not get soiled when it was placed on the cement at M'Vy's feet until the bus came. Long wait, sometimes, Tree knew, before the bus came to pick up passengers.

The pocketbook, sitting square on its four gold knobs. Clink-a-*chunk* in the living room awhile ago when it had been chucked onto the glass-top coffee table. One of the knobs went *chunk* as it hit. It was loose. It sounded in Tree's sleep, clink-a-*chunk*.

M'Vy's coat was flung over the back of the couch. It had white and black stripes, from Mexico. It looked like a hairy blanket to Tree. It was as big as a queen size blanket.

Tree tiptoed through the living room, following the line of discarded clothes. A pair of black suede shoes rested neatly on the seat of the easy chair. They were run over to the outside even without feet in them. There was an archway from the living room that led to a short hall into the kitchen. There were black gloves flung on the floor in the corner outside of the arch. Tree left the living room. She could see a light on in the kitchen. She went in, stopped.

M'Vy was there, stepping out of a pink half-slip under her dress that she kicked into her hand. She was taller than Tree remembered. Darkness and night hovered in a scent of fresh, chill air around her. Alone, it was as if M'Vy were yet outside. What was striking was not so much that she was very tall and alone. She was tall and wide, alone. Big and wide and separate from all other of Tree's loves. M'Vy was big, wide and well boned. Well shaped.

If she had been slender, which she never was, she would have been a dream, Tree thought. As it was, she was a black beauty. She was the woman with the young girl in Brother Rush's country. Tree didn't recall that woman in Rush's place being as big as M'Vy. The size and shape of that woman never entered into what was going on there. She knew the two women had to be one and the same. What she didn't know was whether what she saw and what went on in Rush's place had actually been.

M'Vy's face was tight under skin the color of raw honey. It looked like it had been shined and sprinkled with tiny chocolate chips high on the cheeks. She wore a lavender dress gathered at the shoulders. Old-timey, it fell softly in pale purple folds below her knees. Three-quarter sleeves, like Tree's bathrobe; it was lightweight material, comfortable to wear. M'Vy would perspire from the exertion of going inside and out and climbing on and off buses. Waiting long times at bus stops, waiting at side doors for rain to stop, for snow to stop blowing. She never could stand a lot of clothing. Hardly nothing, maybe some sheer underwear next to her skin.

Coming in silently, unobserved, Tree watched her. M'Vy's chest moved up and down beneath the folds of the dress. She stood by the counter light, sideways and facing away from Tree. She had one hand raised on top of the refrigerator. Tree had often seen her stand that way. Looking around, judging neatness.

Tree always did leave everything just as neat as a pin after each meal, in case Vy came home. M'Vy had to make sure no ragtag lack of discipline had crept into her house. She pronounced the word *dis* i *pline* and she told Tree often enough that *dis* i *pline* was what kept the three of them together.

"You cain't see it," she had told Tree. "You cain't touch it. But it what keep you safe in here. It hold me, working away and coming back to care for yo'w."

Tree's eyes filled with tears. Her throat closed around a large lump of relief, of joy, at having M'Vy home. Yet she had a lost feeling, waiting so long until M'Vy was ready.

Be over soon, Tree thought.

And soon it was over. M'Vy took one last look around. Turning, she saw Tree. "Yes," she sighed. "Tree." Her voice was a singing bird's to Tree. It was high and clear, full of country fresh air.

She flung herself into M'Vy's arms. Vy staggered under Tree's force. Then Vy held her, lifting her off the floor. She swayed with Tree from side to side, smothering the child against her.

What did it matter that Tree couldn't breathe, planted as she was against M'Vy's breast? She would have grown again inside M'Vy if she could have.

Tree closed her eyes. She cried. And cried.

"Poor honey—my baby!" Vy whispered. She didn't loosen her arms around Tree but let Tree's feet touch the floor. She wouldn't let go until Tree was ready.

"Dint call because knew I couldn't get home until way late," Vy said. "You forgive me? Nothin to it. Know I be here every minute if I just could."

Vy's chest shook as, quietly, she began crying along with Tree. Vy made no sound when she cried. Tree looked up to see tears streaming down her face. She let go of Vy and smoothed her hand on the tears. Vy kissed her hand.

"M'Vy," Tree said, "I love you," said haltingly. It was not easy for her to say. Saying it meant she let herself go, it was safe to let go now. Was it?

"I love you, too," Vy told her, clutching Tree's face in her hands. "Okay now, don't cry no more," she said with finality.

"You, either," Tree said.

"All right," Vy said. They pulled apart. Wiped their eyes. Tree located some tissues in a drawer. The tissues made dust as she pulled them out, they were so old.

They stood, wiping their eyes. After a minute, they were giggling. They sat at the table, a pile of tissues between them. They laughed softly at themselves.

"You face all puffy," Tree told Vy. "Lookin like some bee sting you."

Vy smiled, said nothing, sniffing. She had Tree's hands in hers. She patted them; took the wrists and patty-caked Tree's hands. Not saying any words, Vy went through the motions of the rhyme of infants.

Tree giggled. "Makin me a baby!"

They sat there, hand in hand. Vy studied Tree's face as she got hold of herself. "Everything all right, Tree? You got some food left? Knew you'd be running low on food bout now."

"I got some food left," Tree said. "M'Vy?"

"Well, then, everything be all right," Vy said. "Nobody try to break in—you still got the tear gas?"

"Yeah, I got it," Tree said.

"You see nobody follow you home? No boys in here?"

"No!" Tree said. "No." She felt a growing alarm. They

91

were close to dangerous ground. "Nobody botherin me."

"No boys!" Vy said emphatically.

"No'm," said Tree, holding her breath. If Vy would think to ask about Dab and his girls. She never did. Never would she believe that Dab had girls he brought home with him. The thought would never enter her mind.

Think he retarded, Tree thought. But that ain't most of it with Dab. But she sure quick to think I be doin something evil.

Tree suddenly felt angry at M'Vy. It smoldered, then passed to the back of her mind as more pressing considerations came to the fore.

"Dab . . . not feelin so well, you know?" Tree said.

The mood of a few minutes ago had changed. M'Vy stared bleakly around the small kitchen. "Think I make some coffee."

"What time it is?" Tree asked. She glanced at the clock on the stove. "It ain't but three o'clock A.M.," she said.

"Good enough time for coffee," said Vy. She got up to make it.

"It the one thang I cain't do right," Tree said, "makin coffee."

"They lots a *thangs* I *cain't* do right," Vy said. She eyed Tree. She didn't always appreciate Tree's way of speaking words, although she was guilty of the comfortable accent they shared herself. Somehow she felt the comfort of it was something they should get rid of.

"I mean *thing* and *can't*," Tree said. "But M'Vy, no kiddin, Dab be so sick. He can't keep his food down."

Vy stared at Tree. "How long? How long cain't he keep it down?"

"This evening."

"That's nothin but a stomach upset," Vy said.

"No." Tree felt the fear come over her when she

thought of the mystery of her brother's sickness. "He say he in pain. Cain't stand even for me to touch the bed, it so bad."

Vy was silent. Her face seemed to struggle with some distant recollection. "He with some fever?" she asked.

"Yeah," Tree said. "It come and it go with the pain."

"Aching all over?" Vy said.

"Yeah," Tree said.

"He got just the flu."

Tree wouldn't argue. But she didn't think it was a cold or flu that caused such awful pain for Dab.

Let her see for herself in the morning, Tree thought. Cain't . . . can't . . . tell her how it is.

Vy went about making coffee while Tree got up her nerve. Now there was nothing else to talk about but the one thing that made no sense when she put it into words.

Brother Rush, a ghost, Tree thought. How do you say it out loud?

"You believe in ghosts, M'Vy?" she blurted out.

Vy was grinding coffee. She had the glass container of water on the burner. She heard Tree's voice but not the words. "What?" she said.

Tree took a deep breath, another, but it did no good. All at once, she was crying hard, hiding her face in her hands. Just sobbing.

Vy was there, pulling the chair up to her. "Shhh. It's all right, honey. I'm here. I'm goin stay awhile. Maybe two days. Things rough here for you. You too alone."

"No. No," Tree managed to say.

"Dab, being sick. You worryin youself to death," Vy said.

Crying, Tree shook her head, trying to wipe the tears away. She knew how she must look. She was almost choking; her nose was running.

93

"Stop the cryin, Tree," Vy said. "Cryin don't do nobody no good."

"Yeah, it do," Tree said. Her voice was high and whining, out of control. "You not listenin to me!"

"I'm listenin. I'm listenin, Tree," Vy said. "How can I listen with you slobberin yourself?" She giggled nervously in her high, country sound. "What a matter, hon? Tell me, Sweet."

Tree heard her heart beating in her ears, blood rushing, and she took a few gulps of air to calm herself. "Okay. Okay," she said at last. "You might not believe me. But you know I don't lie. You know I'd never in my life lie to you or make up some tales. If you ask me anythang, I'll tell you true."

"I know that," Vy said. "It what I don't think to ask that worry me some," she said.

She smiled, and Tree knew she wasn't serious. Vy had deep dimples when she smiled. She could look like a sexy lady with the dimples, the kind they sang songs about, Tree thought.

"You have a man friend now?" Tree asked her easily, as though they'd just been talking that way. Curiosity came over Tree at any time. "You get a dude," Tree said, "you won't have to ride the bus."

Vy looked at her, appraising her. "What make you think the dude gone have a car? I got a friend."

"You do?" Tree said, astonished that she had accidentally hit upon something cool. "You see him all the time?"

Vy saw the trap and paused a moment. "He don't take me away from yo'w, you and you brother. He just able to see me where I am at most the time."

"I could come round, see you," Tree said. She could not keep the envy from her voice.

"No, you got to care for Dab."

Tree was silent. All resentment evaporated at the mention of her brother. Maybe some could feel evil to a brother they had to care for more than themselves, the way she did for Dab. But she never could. Dab was so much a part of her. She couldn't feel evil about him without feeling the same way about herself inside.

"So you got a *friend*," Tree said. "He one of a few?" Spoken without malice.

Vy understood. "No," she said. "He the only he, named Sylvester Wiley D. Smith. I call him Silversmith." She smiled a secret smile.

"You like him?" Tree asked. "This . . . Silversmith?"

"I do," Vy said. "Nice and kind to me. Give me no trouble. He brang my car by when I need it."

Tree's eyes grew wide. "You got yourself a car! Whyn't you tell somebody! How long you have it?"

"Nothin to it," Vy said casually. "Had it awhile. I need a car for my errands. *They* have a car I could use where I be, but I rather have my own."

"Tell me how long you have it. What kind?" Tree said.

"Nothin, three months. Just a Chivvy. Pretty gray and black, lookin like new but it used. You don't have to get upset about it."

"Three months." Tree's face fell.

"It's nothin!" Vy exclaimed. "What you want me to do, tell you about it, and you not be able to ride in it? Cause I can't be here yet. I got to work where I can and hope for somethin closer to home."

"Yeah. I know," Tree said. "I know it, but he get the car and you and everything. And me and Dab, we got *nothin*."

"That ain't true. It's nothin to it, I tole you. Don't be mouthin," Vy said.

95

"Yeah, why then when you here, we go grocery shoppin on the bus?"

"Cause I don't got it here," Vy said. "I don't trust leavin it on the street. I got too much tied up in it."

"So *he* got it for you," Tree said. "*He* keepin it."

When Vy didn't say a word, she knew it was so. "When I'm gettin to meet this secret Silversmith?" Tree asked.

"Don't go mouthin, Tree. Forget your manners."

"Yeah, I know. We got to have manners and dis *i* pline!" She gave Vy a wicked look. "I know lots of thangs . . . you wouldn't think I know, too," Tree said. Something absolutely hateful twisted her mouth. The idea of a car belonging to M'Vy and Tree not able to see it once made her sick inside. The car was something she had never known she needed badly.

M'Vy shivered. She had the Pyrex of boiling water ready to pour into the filter full of ground coffee. She paused, eyeing Tree. "That a smart-ass smirk you got on your face, girl," she said. "You gettin streetwise, is it?"

"I know lots," Tree shot back at her. She felt as evil as she'd ever dared. Something hard and sharp raced through her, bursting forth with a killing speed. "You beat my brother good when he little, dint you?" she said. "You whumped him and tied him up to the bedpost. Vy. Shi. You sure some mother."

Suddenly Vy's hand holding the glass pot jerked. Hot water spilled, and Vy let go of it. It hit the floor in a burst of exploding glass and searing water. Vy leaped away. Glass flew. Tree jerked her arms, shielding her face. When Tree looked again, the tip of Vy's index finger was a swell of blood dripping in fast beats to the floor.

"Ohhh!" Vy moaned. Her ankles were wet. Places on her dress were soaked.

It wasn't cold wet, either, Tree realized. It had to be

burning wet. "You hurt?" Tree asked her. She hurried for some dish towels in the cabinet.

Vy cringed from Tree. She seemed unaware of hot water over everything; yet her expression registered the pain. She did not notice her finger bleeding steadily now, darkening the side of her dress.

Tree pointed at the streaking stains. "You bleeding, M'Vy. Let me fix it for you." Her anger had evaporated. "Here," she said, taking Vy's hand and pressing a towel to her finger.

Vy pulled her hand away. Her eyes glinted at Tree. "How . . . how . . ." she said.

"Oh. How I know about you tyin up Dab? And you never tell it?" said Tree. "Then it's true? He tellin true?"

"Who he? Dab?" Vy whispered. "Dab tell you that?" She backed against the wall.

"M'Vy, I started to tell you before. We got talking about your boyfriend . . . and your car."

Vy stared at Tree, afraid, as though she were an impossible vision.

"M'Vy, Dab is sick, you know? I mean, real sick. He got to have a doctor or something. You got to believe it. He say the light on him hurt his hands. You got to see his hands. Stuff on 'em, lookin like they been cut up." Tree recalled the ugly scars she'd seen on Dab's hands. She had had no time to even wonder about them until now. "M'Vy, listen," Tree said. And very carefully, "There be a ghost in this house."

Vy's legs quivered. She was sliding. Down the wall she went, sinking to the floor. A shuddering sound escaped her lips. She was on her knees, gazing at Tree.

"You don't have to be afraid," Tree told her. "He won't hurt you." Speaking fast. "It be a male ghost through the table in my little room. See, I had Dab clean

97

off that table so's I could draw? Then he come, dressed so fine. I love him true! Brother Rush be him."

Vy's eyes rolled back. She looked as if she were going to be sick to her stomach. Still, Tree went on.

"I see him first in the street, Brother. Now he come through my round table all the time. Dab and me, we see him through the table, smack in the wood. And that's how I know."

Tree turned her face away. "Know about you back then. Not all," she said. "There's a whole bunch ain't so clear. M'Vy? You want to see him?" She didn't know whether Rush was in the little room. She wouldn't mind taking M'Vy there to see.

"I ain't afraid of it so much no more," Tree said. "I mean him, the ghost. He don't seem to mean no harm." Speaking eagerly, "I'm not positive what he do mean. He young, a little older than me. I care for him."

Vy looked sunken, like a hulking fallen mass of flesh. All of a sudden, she appeared broken down.

Like seein a stranger, Tree thought. She don't look righteous no more.

Tree waited, and finally Vy pulled herself together. She got up, wincing at the pain of cuts. Tree hurried out and back, bringing Vaseline and Band-Aids, all she had. Vy took off her stockings. Wordlessly she rubbed Vaseline into the mean-looking red scratches and burns around her ankles. She winced again and again but said nothing. Then Tree gently spread Vaseline over the injured finger. "It ain't all that bad," she said. "The glass is out of it." She wrapped two Band-Aids around the nail and the jagged line that still oozed blood. "There." She patted M'Vy's shoulder the way she sometimes patted Dab when he was down.

Vy peered at her, hands folded in her lap. She searched Tree's face. "You couldn't possibly remember that. You were too young," Vy said.

"When I was little? Nothin back that far," Tree said. "But how come you don't talk about back then? How come I don't know nobody kin to us anywhere?"

Vy didn't answer directly. "Maybe you did see a ghost." Her voice was shaky, as if she might cry. "I know peoples who has, regularly. They talk to ghosts and confides in em. Maybe so." She sounded fearful, yet resigned. "He my brother, Tree. And he was a grown man. You cain't love him like a *friend*."

"It not your brother," Tree said. "It a ghost."

"It a ghost of Brother Rush," said Vy. "The youngest boy in the family. That my baby brother's name, *Brother*."

"Maybe it was, but it not your brother no more," Tree said. "It eighteen, nineteen—why is that? You think I'm crazy?"

Vy looked quite exhausted. "No," she said simply. "I don't think you crazy, Tree. And we can argue bout what it is all night, and whether, and how come it is. So okay. I don't disbelieve nothin. Let's go see the little room."

Without another word, Tree led the way. She wouldn't dare hope that Rush was there for fear he would not be.

If he ain't there, then am I crazy? But if he be there, then I'm crazy?

CHAPTER
9

The cold of the little room wrapped around Tree. No peculiar light announced the presence of Rush, the ghost. But there was something that was settling in.

They were just inside the door. The door was closed and the room was dark. M'Vy shivered behind Tree; Tree reached back, taking her hand. Vy's hand was wet with cold perspiration. Tree let go and cautiously went forward.

"Shhh!" came from Vy. "Don't move!" whispering. She was scared to death of what she might see in the dark. "Oooh. Oooh!" she moaned.

Tree found the table and reached out over it with both hands. She kept her eyes closed, which made her feel that the dark was softer and less fearsome, and she could concentrate better. She felt around in the air over the table and found a small space that was bone-chilling, sending imaginary ice shards up to her elbows. Cold came so very far to reach her.

Cold, sun-time, she thought.

Sunshine with little warmth was what it was like. She knew sunlight in the feeling up her arms. Cold sun. April, with sun that was warming. She knew her feet were in the sun. Somewhere. Her feet were quite small.

"M'Vy, see?" she said, through the dark. "We just got

100

here too soon. He on his way, coming in the table. Rush be here, and I'll be a baby-child.

"M'Vy, come over here!" Tree said urgently. "He coming *now!*"

"Turn on a light. Oh, please, turn on a light!" Vy cried.

Tree opened her eyes. The dark of the room faded in a peculiar, gossamery glow. Rush settled.

He was big as life. He was as handsome as he'd ever been. Tree couldn't imagine where he'd bought a suit like that. Fleetingly she wondered how much it had set him back.

Rush was there, and the space he held in one gloved hand like an oval mirror was April, with bright spring sunshine. The space grew and grew; it took over the ghostly figure of Rush himself. He had moved. He was in a seated position. There was somebody with him.

Tree was standing by the hood of a car. She could see the reflection of sunlight on the windshield. Branches commenced moving. In the reflection was a cold sun, racing.

How can this be, she thought. She was in the little room, looking into the scene of mysterious light. She could see Rush just as clear. He wore beautiful yellow suede gloves; his hands clutched the steering wheel. Brother drove fast. There was a child with him.

"Tree, turn on the light."

"What? M'Vy, can't you see him? It's Brother. It's Rush, the ghost!"

"I can feel it! Hush! Be a ghost, hush, turn on a light!"

The door of the little room opened. A shaft of light illuminated Dab. Tree had turned to see. Dab was holding onto the door to hold himself up. With the other hand, he held his robe closed.

101

Why cain't he wear a tie-belt? Tree was aware of thinking.

Stooped over slightly, he was weak but not hurting too terribly. She could tell how he was feeling. If he could get his robe on, then the pain was not so great. Dab's legs were weak and shaking. She couldn't recall when he'd had a good, square meal.

Reluctantly Tree turned away from Dab. She looked again into bright, cool sunshine. It had taken over the round table and all the space above it.

Dab shoved past Vy; the door closed, and all was dark again. Tree and Dab stood together, absolutely still in the dark of the little room.

Vy couldn't hold back her terror. She didn't know what to do. She couldn't see a thing. So she waited.

She knew there was something. Silently, she asked the Lord to protect her.

She could feel it, the way they say you always know when it comes, unsettling the air. Ghost.

Tree observed. There were two children in the car with Brother Rush. There was the girl beside Rush. Next to her was the boy, sitting on his bony knees. Tree, the girl, was standing on the seat.

She had on a sky-blue dress with lace at the bodice and wrists. She had taken off her white shoes and blue socks. She had kicked them on the floor at the boy's feet. The boy took up her socks; then he rolled down the window.

Hey! Brother yelled. He was driving fast, and he slowed down. Hey, roll it up, son. You wait; it getting warmer fast. When it warmer, you can roll the window down.

She knew what the boy wanted to do. She had her body pressed behind Brother's shoulder as he drove. If for any reason he had to stop short, she would not fall forward. His shoulder would brace her.

She started hitting the boy with the flat of her hand on the temple and on his ear. She had seen the woman do it.

The boy grinned, staring straight ahead out the window. He rolled the window all the way down. He bunched her socks in his hand and flung them out the window.

Hey! You had to do it, dint you? And I taken you for a ride to prove to her that you good and decent! Brother was angry.

The boy rolled the window up. He grinned wildly and was satisfied with himself. She stopped hitting him. Her blue socks. She didn't care that they were gone. And she forgot them. She was happy to have nothing on her feet. Barefoot, she discovered cold places on the seat when she pranced up and down on the tips of her toes. There was a warm spot next to Brother. She wiggled her toes, stuck her leg straight out — her leg was bare — and felt warm air from the heater. She put her foot on the round knob Brother moved when the car changed speed. The gear-shift knob was cold unless Brother kept his hand on it. Gloves kept his hands warm and turned the knob warm.

She kicked and pranced. She folded her hands on top of Brother's head.

Hey! said kindly, laughing. Don't you go mess up my *wig*.

She didn't look to see whether the boy was watching. She could feel him next to her. Always when just the two of them were in the car with Brother, the boy was next to her. When the woman was in the car, she had to sit on the woman's lap. And the boy would be in the backseat, out of sight.

She liked standing, with no shoes, bare legs growing chilly now. Her feet looked yellow, were quite cool. She didn't much care. They were flying in the car down the

103

gray strip of road. There was sun, then shade in stripes and circles on the road. They went up high on the hills, and they went down.

Have to take you back now, kids, Brother told them. His face changed. All smiling was gone. The fun had vanished.

She looked at the boy. He was staring straight ahead.

Give us another hour, she tried to tell Brother. She never could get the words right, just like the boy couldn't. One day she would get them right. And she already knew what an hour felt like. She wanted to be riding in the car for more time and stopping along the road. She saw some big animals in the fields, looking warm. It might be getting warm outside in the sun. They could stop and drink out of a bottle of Kool-Aid Brother had made just for her and the boy. Brother had his own bottle under the seat. It looked like water with lemon peel in it.

She and the boy threw a fit. She kicked and jumped up and down, screaming and pretending to cry. The boy beat his head on the glove compartment. He hurled himself on the dashboard, then on the door. She threw herself at the boy and against Brother. She was dangerously close to causing him to slap her down.

She sprawled across the steering wheel. Brother slapped her legs.

Get out of the way!

His hands in the gloves couldn't hurt her. Brother wouldn't try to hurt her. He was warning her, was what he was trying to do.

Finally he did what they wanted. He took them deep in the country to the Bryan Park. He showed them the shelter where the church had outings twice a year. The outings began after church on Sunday and lasted well past midnight. The social would be topped off with a moonlight picnic. Long tables of food. Children so over-wrought by night and starlight, they threw up the delicious floating-island dessert.

She had not been a witness to such an extraordinary social event. But she had heard about it from the boy. Once, when he was tied up, he had talked of nothing else. He'd heard other boys talking. He wanted to go to a moonlight picnic, but they never let him.

Brother stopped the car in sunlight in a valley with hills around it.

This is the Jacoby Valley, he told them. Owned by old man Jacoby. All this region is private land. Man is stone rich.

They got out of the car. Sun was warming as they walked across the road. The boy climbed to the top of a wood fence. Brother lifted her and she sat up there, too. They waited to see animals up close. There came a horse, huffing at them and swinging its long head. It veered and went off into the distance. Far away was a farmhouse with barns. The air was so still, they could hear chickens and animal sounds.

Brother brought them Kool-Aid in jelly glasses. He took out his jar of white liquid with lemon peel.

Gin-gin-gin, said the boy.

Engine, she thought, and tried to say it. The boy laughed and laughed at her. She hit him on the head.

Brother drank out of the jar. They drank Kool-Aid while sitting on the fence. It was fun. She loved the sun and freshness on her toes and legs. She rubbed her feet one against the other. She laughed and drank the Kool-Aid. Red Kool-Aid, tasting overly sweet, but good.

Brother pulled a small sack out of his coat and shook ginger snaps into her hand and into the boy's hand. They drank red sweetness and ate tart ginger snaps. They were so happy on the fence. Brother drank from his jar and filled his cheeks with six ginger snaps, three on each side. It wasn't possible, but Brother counted them as he popped them in his cheeks. She and the boy shrieked with laughter. Brother grinned at them as the ginger snaps melted in his mouth.

Brother stared out over the empty field. There were no animals now. The baby-girl saw a swell of shade under trees way down the field. There was bare earth in the shade. Animals might have rested there. She thought of crying out that she had to see animals. Maybe Brother could find some for her to touch. Especially horses and cows. There was a breeze where there was shade. It caught tree leaves in silvery light.

Gone rain, Brother murmured. Leaves turn them backs over silver and rain every time by evening.

His murmuring was another part of the day. The sound felt as if it were shining on her skin.

It wasn't yet noon. She squirmed on the fence until Brother sat her down in the grass at his feet. The grass pricked the back of her legs. She scooted up against the fence. Nice, sitting with bare legs sticking out under her dress. She had dropped cookie crumbs down her front. She wiped them away, leaving wet streaks. Her fingers were sticky red with Kool-Aid.

Brother leaned down and brushed her good. There. You don't sit still, you'll spill your drink. Be more trouble than you worth, Sweet.

Sweet was her name that no one used very much. Brother used it and it sounded friendly. He sat down, back to the fence, the way she was sitting. He was between her and the boy. She leaned forward, taking a look at the boy. He was staring around at everything. All around were valley fields and surrounding hills against the sky. They sat. They heard a far-off whistle.

The boy stared at the road, where the car sat, red Buick, blood-red and big.

106

Brother got up, strode to the car and opened the trunk. He took out a hat, and he put it on. It was a straw hat, big, like a farmer's. It covered his face with shade. She saw how easy it was that shade was made. Brother was so careful to keep his arms and neck covered. He arranged the hat and the collar of his shirt. Carefully pulled his cuffs. He made certain his socks covered his legs where the pants didn't reach when he sat down again.

Soon Brother lay on his back. He let lie the bag of ginger snaps. Quickly the boy got hold of them and hid them behind him. She saw him do it.

Brother had the hat over his face now. It made shade on his ear. The glass jar lay on its side next to him. All it had in it was a small amount of liquid at the bottom and lots of lemon peels. Once Brother was snoring, the boy took the jar and drank everything left at the bottom.

She told him he oughtn't to do that. She crawled over, careful not to touch Brother, and hit the boy on his ear. She didn't much like hitting. She did it because the woman did it. She sat, finishing the Kool-Aid. Finished, she looked at the boy. She inquired if he would take her to the bathroom. She had to go. He turned away. She sat, and soon she went in her pants. There, in the grass, it was warm wet under her at first. Then the wet became uncomfortable. She thought she'd better go walking in the sun. She stood up in her pretty dress. She forgot about ginger snaps and Kool-Aid. She would walk down the road.

Hee! Hee! You peed on yourself! the boy said.

Brother stirred but did not wake. She could detect a warm, thick smell on Brother's breath.

She whined at the boy to come with her. He got up. He walked with her to the side of the road, pointed where she must walk beside the road. He threw stones in the road. She walked on the side in the grassy places with bare feet. She told the boy to take his shoes off. Throw them away, she told him in her child words, just as he had thrown her socks away. She remembered the socks now and looked all up and down the road for a point of blue. The road was gray. The boy wouldn't throw his shoes away.

They walked down the road together. They could look back, seeing the car and Brother. Brother and the car got smaller and small, but they were still there. Then they sat on the far side of a curve in the road. Suddenly the boy had a terrible stomach ache. Sweat popped out all over his face and neck. He was trembling. Saliva fell in strings from his mouth. He held his stomach with both hands. He could no longer stand. And fell, whipping his legs back and forth on the ground. There were grass stains all over his tan pants. The woman would tie him up for dirtying his pants.

He lay panting, holding his stomach. He didn't seem like the boy anymore. He was old, hurting. He panted like he couldn't breathe. She began to cry.

CHAPTER
10

It was a long kind of time. Through it, she watched the boy sleep. She had stopped crying. Her underwear was nearly dry again. But she smelled. She could smell herself. She woke the boy. It took him time to know where he was.

Is it hurting? she asked him. His mouth turned down. He bit his lip. For an instant, he looked like he would have the worst crying. Then his face straightened in a brown mask.

Carefully he got up. They walked back around the bend. He took off his jacket and gave it to her. She trembled with the fresh day, shrouded in dampness.

You want me carry you, girl? he asked. He could hardly manage to speak the words.

She could walk. I can walk, she told him as best she could. Her feet were cold and yellow. The cold climbed and settled below her knees. Smiling, she thanked him for the jacket. They held hands. That is, she took hold of his hand and he allowed her to. She swung his arm over and back. He let her do that. And she was glad his hurting seemed to have disappeared.

They were tiny beside the long, slow shimmer of gray road. Bright light from above fell over them from the high-riding blue. It made them seem to rise on the green roadside. Their walking was a day rhythm in the midst of quiet light.

They were back, standing over Brother Rush. His shirt collar was unbuttoned. He had covered the exposed skin of his neck and throat with a handkerchief. Asleep again, his hands in the soft suede gloves were crossed over his silver belt. They saw his fingers twitch; and each time the coffee-smooth of his face erupted in knots.

Loving the pretty gloves, she leaned over, pulled at one finger. Pulled the next gloved finger. Suede was soft, so tan and new. The woman had black kid gloves she wore to church and the girl was not allowed to try on.

The boy thought pulling fingers was a good game. He pulled the glove off Rush's other hand. Brother began to stir. Then both gloves were off. Brother's bare hands clenched and trembled. They stared at his hands. They forgot about the gloves. They dropped them on the ground.

The boy was first to turn away. But fascinated by what he had seen, he looked again. His eyes were big and round, frightened.

She stared at Rush's bare hands. Sucked in her breath in shocked surprise. The skin was thick with sores and white-looking scars. There were brown marks on the backs of his hands, and red sores. The marks and sores were not like what the woman made on the boy when she whipped him with a stick. They were not from any kind of beating, the girl knew. Ugly, sore-looking hands. Painful hands, full of sickness.

All at once, Brother sat up, wide awake. He fumbled for his gloves and angrily swatted at the two of them. You, kids! But that was all. Breathing hard, he put the gloves on. His hat had rolled away. He cringed and held his face away from the sun until he had the hat back on.

Why'd you let me fall asleep out here! he said. He got up. Pain hit him in the stomach. He doubled over for a moment, the way the boy had done awhile ago.

She mentioned to him that the boy had been sick. But he lurched away toward the car. Yo'w . . . he said. Yo'w come here!

They hurried to the car. The boy stuffed the ginger-snap sack in his pocket. He thought to bring Brother's Mason jar. He was so fond of the liquid mixed with lemon peel at the bottom, and the lemony odor that floated out on the air. He found the lid and screwed it on the jar, hiding the bottle under his jacket.

Brother made both of them sit in the backseat. They could see his face in the rearview mirror. They saw his eyes fill up with tears; then the tears would melt away. The girl heard him suck in his breath, the way the woman had done when she had a deep cavity in one of her teeth.

Enough, Brother muttered. No more. No more. Oh, Lord. Lord, the light!

He slumped behind the wheel in a state of nerves and agitation. Breathing hard, sucking in his breath as if every other minute a ferocious wave of something awful hit him.

Awful pain, she decided. Every other minute his hands pained him; and the way he moved his head, his face hurt him. His face had become red and raw. When they left home, Brother's face had been as ordinary as the man Ken's. Just brown and fatherly. Ken, the father, worked today. He worked every day, even Sunday, for at least part of the day.

Brother fumbled in his pocket, took out a small container. He slipped something from the container in his mouth. And leaned back, mumbling to himself, Cain't take no more. Oh, God, no more . . .

After a time, Brother could move again. His facial coloring seemed to have toned down. The hat shielded his face well.

She said, Why you wearin a hat in the car? In this heat in here?

Brother made no reply but started the car. She watched the gloved hands holding the steering wheel like it was a red-hot poker bent in a circle.

You see 'em, see his hands? she asked the boy. He had his face in the Mason jar, sniffing sweet fumes. He didn't bother to answer her.

Still within the ghost time, they were at the woman's house in a blink of an eye. The girl was on the porch swing with the woman. She could hear the boy, thump-thumping upstairs. The windows were open and up on screens all over the house.

The thump-thumping was like day, which came and went, like rain, and like the pump in the basement of the house, thumping on and off in the flash-flood time of spring. Spring was now. It could flash flood at anytime.

Who knew this? Did the girl know this? It was Tree who knew, who was emerging now from the girl.

Gone be a warm day, ninety or more, I bet, the woman said brightly to Brother, who had been there once and had come back again. He was standing in the shade near the porch. There was a young maple tree right by the steps. Brother stood there, his hat in the leaves.

Why you over there, Brother? the woman said. Whyn't you come on up here?

Brother came quickly up on the porch.

He got a sunburn, the boy had said when they were in the car. Now the girl said it.

He got him sunburned, she said in her small voice, saying parts of words she knew. They were not always the right words. They were what she knew and she used them for everything. The woman didn't know that. Neither did Brother.

The boy knew. Upstairs, he thumped harder. He heard

her say, Let me down. Down. I want down, and he knew she was talking about Brother's face. The boy knew a lot.

See you got your straw out, the woman said to Brother. She let the girl slide off her lap, for the child had said she wanted down. The girl scrambled up again, on Brother's lap this time. She was whimpering, saying, Let me down, but meaning something entirely different.

Tree was emerging from the child. She was coming out of it. She could feel it happening.

I'm here in this place, she thought. What has happened. Something will happen that took place when I was here before.

Will you pick me up some books? the woman asked. Tree had heard her ask for number books once before.

I have to go. I got to hurry, Brother told her. Tree saw his face go still. He had hidden an expression of pain and sadness.

The girl cried out. She raised her arms to Brother.

I've seen her do that before, Tree thought. Brother will put her on his head a minute, before he leaves.

And it happened as Tree had seen it happen before. Brother swung the child down again into the woman's lap.

Got to go, Sweet, Brother told the child. With ghostly suddenness, he was in his car. Tree was with him, almost under his skin, as if she meant to drive the car herself. She was so close to Brother, she shared some of his pain and sadness. She knew how to keep it hidden.

Tree had an urgent desire to get things over with. The place of these people was beginning to come apart for her. She needed soon to get back to her own place, her own people again.

Where we going, Brother? Tree said. He could not hear her.

In this dream-place, or whatever it was she was in, Brother was no longer the eighteen- or nineteen-year-old handsome dude she'd first seen on the street and then through the table. Now he was old enough to be her uncle, which he was, or even her father, which he wasn't. In the car with her now, he was a middle-aged man. But he had on the same clothes, the same beautiful suit and shirt, as he had the first time she'd seen him. Two ages of the same ghost, wearing the same suit.

And she didn't know why.

Always got to run errands for her, shoot, she heard Brother say to himself. We gone be late for the game!

The car was flying. It screeched to a halt at his home across town. Tree knew he lived alone. They were in the house. All was dark. Window blinds were green, drawn down against sunlight. The rooms were still and shadowy.

Why won't he turn on a light? Tree thought.

He put a night light in a wall socket behind an easy chair. By this faint light, he contemplated his dim reflection in the mirror. Face, ghosty, barely visible. His hands fluttered to his face. Cain't stand no more, he moaned.

There was pain in his face and hands and arms. It was down his back. Tree couldn't imagine how he lived with so much pain day after day. For he was awfully sick with something.

Brother's home was not much of a home. Just mostly empty, dark space. There was but one picture in the whole place. It was on his dresser. A framed photograph of ten or so people all standing facing the camera. Behind them was a shiny convertible. There was a short, thin, older man in the middle. There were four young men on one side of him and six women on the other. The men and women, at various stages of youth. Ten children, Tree counted. One would be the woman on the porch

114

swing. Tree recognized Brother as the youngest-looking boy. She had never seen the other children. The faces of the remaining three boys in the photograph had been Xd out. Big Xs across their bodies.

Staring in the mirror, Brother had forgotten what he came for.

In the drawer, Tree told him. Lookit, there are the number books she want. Just get them for her.

He couldn't hear her talking. But just before he left the house, he remembered. He got the books and hurried out. He had to meet friends in the next town. He would pick up one person here, not far away. And they would all drive to Cincinnati to the night ball game. Cincinnati Reds at the beginning of the season. Brother was faithful and wouldn't miss one night game. He had a season ticket. Drinking, talk and laughter, chicks, was what the Reds game was about. Down by the river. Forgot all their troubles. Brother took an umbrella against the strong sun. His friends no longer made a joke about it.

Can I go, too? Tree asked him. Never been no ball game before.

Only the men went. Brother didn't bother mentioning this fact to the woman with the girl. She never asked to go.

Tree was in the car going fast. Brother was late for the one pickup in the town. He went to the northside, where there was a ball-bearing plant. Standing on the street near the plant entrance was a man waiting, as Brother brought the Buick to a screeching halt beside him. The man looked alarmed at how close Brother had come to his feet. But he didn't flinch.

He was in the car, taking Brother's place. I'll drive, the man said.

Tree knew the voice; found it soothing. Who are you? she asked him, who you belong to?

115

Brother slid over, not looking at the man. Nor did the man look at Brother.

He drove. You look sick, he said to Brother. Brother made no comment back. Neither Brother nor the man knew Tree was there.

She cried out, Listen! I'm talking to you!

They wouldn't answer. She gave it up. The man drove. The back of his neck was clean-shaven. His hair above the collar was crinkly and dark. He smelled freshly shaved. The plant must've had a shower room.

Got to take some books to her, and we already late, Brother was saying.

I'll bring em to her on the way back. She can't do nothing with them tonight, the man said.

Tree thrilled at the sound of his voice. It quieted her and was soothing.

She'll be mad if she don't get them books first thing in the morning, Brother said.

Be back by five A.M., the man said. She don't get on her route before ten.

What if we don't make it back? You know. What if we get too simple and have to stay the night? Brother said. Or if I get sick like I do sometimes after an outing.

You worry, and you only her brother, the man said. He laughed. I'm her husband; you let me take care of her. We coming home after the game. I got to work tomorrow.

So do I, Brother said, weakly.

So the man is the father of the girl and boy, Tree thought. The woman is my mother and the man is my father. The girl is me and the boy is my brother.

It was the first time she had thought it all out.

Be bad if Johnny Nab stop us and find these books, Brother said.

Better place, under the seat, the father said. Brother stuffed the books in the space beneath the front seats.

The father had to move his legs and take his foot off the gas so Brother could maneuver.

There. Done, Brother said.

The father tooled the big Buick through the south town. On the outskirts, he drove like a maniac, the way Brother did. He was in a hurry to get to Wilberforce and then on down the highway to Cincinnati.

You a stone driver, Tree told him, proud of him. But if he was her father, why couldn't she remember him? Why didn't she know anything about him?

He drove fast over the curving, twisting country road. Tree wasn't scared. She was watchful, amused by the flood of flowing colors and the dark and light of day that streamed by them. She had her eyes on the road when a car appeared out of nowhere, going in the opposite direction. Sparkling sun glinted on its windshield. It must have been almost at once that another object appeared, but on their side. She failed to see it and the man failed to see. She'd been watching Brother and the way he seemed to be pretending to sleep. But his eyes were open. She saw this in a casual glance in the split second before disaster was on them. Suddenly Brother lifted his arms in a shield. Terror twisted his mouth. But then, in a breath of a second, he made an act of will. He never warned the father driving.

As the car passed, they came out of deep shade into blinding sunlight. Right before them was a woman on a red bicycle. The terrible suddenness of her position in their path had the impact on them of a tank or a freight train in the wrong place. A tornado right there in the road where you couldn't miss it. Her rightful place was on the other side of the road with the oncoming cars. Instead, she was a deadly shade on a blood-red bike. Startled, like a flushed deer. She had on a yellow play suit. It blended with the brilliance of the sunshine.

Just unlucky, crossed Tree's mind, in that suspended

117

moment when they in the car and the stranger on the bicycle were snared by a tragic day. All was still, poised and suspended, as though time had taken a swallow. The red bike was a still shot. The terror-stricken stranger had her feet balanced on the pedals. Tree noticed she had small feet in brown sandals.

The father didn't have time to choose the ditch at the side of the road. All he could think of was getting the enormous car away from the young woman. Couldn't bear the thought of it smashing into her, all that blood! Instinctively he slammed his foot on the gas pedal. Swerving, the car became airborne, missing the ditch entirely. He had no chance to warn Brother to hold on. There was an open field; they were going to come down in it, perhaps blowing all their tires.

Brother was not braced for the crash. But he had been first to realize what would happen and yet he had not informed the father. Tree had no time to brace herself for the impact.

I'm not here—am I? she thought.

She was in the car, seeing everything in minute detail in the second or two it took for all of it to happen.

They were in the air. Brother's door flew open. Brother was falling out; leaning, leaning out. The father reached for him in a convulsive clutching, but his hand closed on thin air.

Brother leaped high; his eyes were closed. The car door swung in as the car dived.

No! said Tree.

The door caught Brother beneath his chin. His head snapped back. His eyes opened in astonishment. Tree heard a sharp crack. Brother spun through the air. He was a rag doll, falling.

The car took forever to come down. But it was going to crash.

Let me out! Tree, thinking, not even time to holler it.

Not supposed to be here!

She threw herself through the upholstery, through the trunk of the car. She was pushing through the round table, fighting her way back into her own place. Forcing, willing herself, she was getting to where she ought to be.

In the little room. Panting, trying to breathe, she thought her lungs would burst. Tree was holding onto Dab. She had her arms wrapped around his waist. He held her by the shoulders. For a moment, she couldn't think, couldn't speak. Then, "Dab. Dab," she whispered.

"Yeah? Yeah?" he said.

She breathed hard. "It was awful, just awful. But you were there—you saw what happened."

"I was tied," he told her glumly. But he spoke in his brave, manly voice. "Me, all tied. Yeah."

"Oh, no!" Tree gasped. For it was never the same for the two of them. They might go at the same time through the space Rush held, but they saw and heard and felt individually.

She kept a close watch on Rush through the table. Still there, he was a young man holding sunlight and springtime in his free hand. The other hand he held up to his ear, listening. His eyes were dead eyes.

Why he standing up so dead? Tree thought.

He was a young ghost through the table. But he was a man old enough to be her father when Tree had been in the car. A man, killed.

Dab trembled with her weight against him. He was too weak to hold her. She let him go and wrapped her arms around herself.

M'Vy was there in the dark. She found the courage to

turn on a light when she realized they had come to.

Tree spun on her when the light went on. "You close the barn too late," she said. "He already going. See how he fading?" Tree watched as Brother and his grace of mysterious light seemed to fade out in the distance.

"Tree. I ain't seen not one thing. Not in the table. Not anywhere," Vy said.

"You had to see him," Tree said, but without conviction.

"But I'm not saying you and Dabney didn't see my baby brother. He didn't cross over for me to see him. Oh, I know ghosts," M'Vy said. "Lord. He came for the two of yo'w."

She went to them. She touched Tree lightly, then folded her in, holding tightly. Gently Vy stroked Dab on his shoulder. It was her heartfelt attempt to be kind to him. She knew what she had done to him in the past. Her only boy child was born silly. Had half a mind. It made her sick to think about it. She couldn't help it; he made her sick to death. She blamed him for his own half-wittedness. Knew she was wrong. How could a mother feel that way about her own child? But she did; she had from the time she realized he was going to be so different. Dab turned her stomach. Always had.

Tears welled in her eyes. She bowed her head in shame.

CHAPTER
11

Everything happened so fast, Tree didn't get the chance to talk to M'Vy about the car wreck in Rush's place. She wanted to ask, did it truly happen? Did you brother die?

But Dab had collapsed in the hallway outside the little room. Afraid of the little room and what she could sense, feel, but could not see there, M'Vy had hurried them out. And Dab had keeled over.

Tree had the sensation of him slipping fast. He had been right beside her; then he was like a thin column of air rushing to the floor. She moved to stop his fall, but she was too late.

"Get him into bed," M'Vy urged. Tree was pulling at him, trying to lift him.

"Don't! Don't!" Dab shouted at her. "Who! Who, un-huh?" he said in a frenzy of wild talking. "The clean water walking all over. Throw me in the clean water!"

He whipped his body around on the floor in a fit. His eyes rolled back. Vy held his tongue until Tree could go fetch a washcloth. Then Vy rolled it and placed it between his teeth so he wouldn't swallow his tongue.

"His temperature up high. His pulse racing," M'Vy said, clasping his hand and wrist. Tree had never seen a big woman like her move so smoothly doing her job. But each time she touched Dab, he hollered in pain. Finally she gritted her teeth against his hollering and picked him up. She heaved him over her shoulder with his arms pinned under him. With the washcloth in his mouth, Dab couldn't cry out too loudly. He was too weak to kick.

Vy got him in bed with the covers pulled up to his chin.

"Now. We make a search," she said. Dab was out of it, not hearing much beyond his own moaning.

"A search?" Tree asked.

"We search the whole room," Vy told her. She had taken the cloth from Dab's mouth. He had calmed down and appeared to be moaning himself to sleep.

Tree had never searched for anything, except at church a few times when there were Easter-egg hunts. She had been a little girl then. How long ago had that been, she wondered.

She and Vy searched Dab's room while he slept. It wasn't like searching for a mislaid belt or lost watch stem. Once Tree had had to get down on the floor and practically comb it to help M'Vy find her watch stem. Found it, too.

"Don't believe you eyes," Vy told her now. "Believe what you can or cain't feel. Feel under the chair. Feel behind the bureau. Sure's I'm me, we'll find something under or in back of."

Tree found a stash under the windowsill. Two envelopes of pills. M'Vy found MJ taped to the back of the headboard.

No wonder he lay in bed half his life, Tree thought. "He a stone junkie?" Tree wanted to know. She felt bad for him inside.

"Naw, he not," Vy said. "He just want to shut down some pain and feeling crazy, he don't know why. Tree, he a long story." Vy sounded sad, resigned. "Not the time for it now. But he don't know the meaning of what he do. Lord."

She sounded tired, but she searched the room thoroughly. She searched under the carpet. When she had finished, they had a stash to last Dab a month, Tree guessed. Maybe two months.

M'Vy kept watch over Dab. She stayed with him most of the day. Staying with him made her feel better, less ashamed of herself. She would gently rouse him and take his temperature. With Tree watching every move, she would spoon chicken soup down his throat.

"Can't you give him some medicine?" Tree asked.

"Not yet," Vy said. "I have to make sure I give him the right thing," she said. "They got so many new medicines, never know how they work with the drugs in his system."

Now and then Vy would touch Dab's arms or his neck; his hands. Hands that were scarred and mottled. Dab would heave up at her touch and go crazy and vomit the soup on himself.

"What wrong with him?" Tree asked finally. "M'Vy, he don't eat nothing in so long."

"Better he don't for now, you see what happens," she said.

Late Sunday afternoon, Vy made phone calls. "You go get supper," she told Tree to get rid of her. "What food you got, we'll eat, you and me. No, wait. Let me think." Vy had her palm covering the speaker of the phone. Then she lifted it. "Wait a minute," she said into the phone, like the person was somebody she knew real well. "No," she said to Tree, covering the mouthpiece again, "don't cook nothing. We'll be out. We'll go head and eat out someplace."

"Yeah? Yeah?" Tree said, sounding the way Dab would say it. "We be out . . . shopping."

Vy wouldn't take the time to say. She shooed Tree away and closed the door to her bedroom. Tree could hear her on the phone, but not the words.

How we eat out, Tree wondered, with Dab so sick? Who going to carry him down the street? You kidding? If she planning to leave him here by himself, I won't go! She felt her anger rising; it overwhelmed her, and she stood there trembling until her fury at M'Vy passed. It left her frightened, it had come on her so fast.

She went to her brother. She found Dab lying on his back. He looked crazy, gross-out, like from *The Exorcist*. His eyes looked about to fall out of their sockets. He was crazy-grinning with yellow teeth. Eyes narrowed and were evil. Tree didn't want to go near him. Dab lifted his head to watch her. Any minute, she was sure his head would start spinning. But he flopped back on the pillow. At once, he lifted his head again, his eyes riveted on her and his face contorted with pain.

"Don't do that, Dab. Just lie still," she said from her place against the wall.

He muttered to himself. Words had sound but no sense.

"Dab, you hungry? You want to try some more soup?"

He mumbled. The sheet shook as if he were freezing under it. Dab did look as dry and hot as a desert. She couldn't believe how thin he'd become in just one day.

Not only one day, it's been going on for days, and I didn't see it. Too close to him. I'm to blame. No. Am I spose to take care of everything?

She slipped away, going into the living room to calm herself. M'Vy was still on the phone. Tree turned on the TV and stared at a stock-car race; then fast cutting to golf, until the pictures wouldn't stay in focus and her eyes got heavy. She was sleeping fitfully but on the edge of a deep, exhausted sleep when the doorbell rang. It pulled her back. She slid off the couch, wide-eyed, but not fully awake. She was moving, and when she got to the door, M'Vy was right behind her.

"I open it?" she asked huskily, still with her sleep voice.

"Yes, open it," Vy told her.

Opening the door, unlocking the locks. She concentrated and was back to herself.

There stood a man filling the whole space at the threshold. He was tall and big, the way M'Vy was. He was darker in color than M'Vy. There was a red hue to his dark skin.

Like somebody red-color some chocolate, Tree thought. Maybe chocolate left in the path of sundown. Smooth skin.

He had black, silky eyebrows and black hair with some gray through it. His hair was Fro'd. It looked like it had been cut in the past few days. He had big features for a big man. Tree looked him over hard, she couldn't help it. She hadn't ever seen anybody just like him. He wore a brown suit with a white stripe, and a white shirt that made his neck turn black against the whiteness. Tree thought the effect was beautiful. He held a brown felt beret in his hand.

Now what kind gone wear a tam-berey, Tree wondered. Swiftly her mind flowed. You see some girl scouts wear them.

She searched her mind and remembered Mr. Sawallow who taught industrial arts. He wore a tam-berey. Mr. Sawallow was a white gentleman, that was the best way to describe him—a gentleman. The dudes made all kinds of things in his shop classes they weren't supposed to. He pretended he didn't notice. Girls who took shop said Mr. Sawallow was respectful and kind, showing the dudes something. They all laughed at him for trusting them like they were all the same. They didn't dislike him and they didn't treat him rough. They thought he was a fool for trusting all of them equally without a single one of them proving by test and error that he or she was trustworthy. Deep down they suspected Sawallow thought they were all the same because they were all one race. This they resented with a passion.

A black anybody know better than that, Tree thought. All white folks ain't alike—are they?

Dab trusted people, she had time to think, as Vy gently took her shoulders and planted her on the side, out of the way, so the man standing there could come inside. Tree must've been standing there staring at him like a fool, herself.

"Teresa, this is my friend, Sylvester," M'Vy said, using Tree's proper name as the man walked in.

He had such a wonderful smell about him. After-shave cologne, Tree suspected. She couldn't take her eyes off him; managed to say, "Pleased to meet you."

"Everybody call her Tree," Vy said to Sylvester. "You know, shorten Teresa and what d'ya get? But she so tall, like me, she is like a Tree, anyhow," Vy said, almost as bubbly as a girl.

"Glad to meet you, Tree," Sylvester said. He had a real nice voice, Tree thought. It was deep and husky, like a blues singer. And he was big, just the way she pictured the best father to be. "Call me Silversmith," Sylvester told her. "That what everybody call me."

"Okay!" Tree said. "Silversmith."

"That's it. You got it," he said and let go of her hand. Hand so warm, Tree had been hardly aware he had hold of hers. Nice, neat fingernails he had.

"Well, make yourself at home," M'Vy said.

He looked around. Tree couldn't get over how big and manly he was.

Some men just big, she thought. But they don't move like they be careful of you or what all that strength can do if it knock into something. Silversmith know how to move and be smooth.

"You got a nice place," he said to M'Vy in an easy voice. "A nice home."

"Try to make it that way," Vy said, leading the way to the living room. They went in. Tree gave a glance once toward the little room beforehand, and then away from it. She didn't give all the questions she needed to ask M'Vy a chance to come welling up inside her to trouble her.

"Me not being home," Vy said, "well, I depend so much on Tree to take care of things."

"Know you do all you can," Sylvester told her. "Tree not like most kids these days, thinking just themselves," he said, looking kindly at Tree.

She managed to smile. How your kids? was what she wanted to say but thought better of it. Supposing his kids, if he had any, were all strung out and shiftless?

"Silversmith has a son," Vy told Tree, almost reading her mind.

"You meet him sometime, know you like him," Vy went on. Shyly, she smiled at Silversmith. Nice looks passed between them.

Tree felt comfortable with Silversmith and M'Vy. She could imagine the three of them together for all time, the way they say it in fairy tales. She smiled wryly to herself at the thought, for she knew better than to dream. And yet she could not help herself as her mind slid easily away until she no longer understood what they were saying. She didn't even try as she swung into a warm reverie. She made up her own words and pictures to please herself. Words and pictures by Sweet Tree. Silversmith and M'Vy together in the living room with neatness, and a book by Warren Miller, provided by Sweet Tree. They would stay in the house as long as Tree needed them to. Even Brother Rush would stay.

Tree thought, Sweet, whispers Brother Rush. Naw, that ain't it. It, Sweet whispers, Brother Rush. Brother Rush!

Somewhere inside, Tree cried out, longing to be in that place she had seen, where she was forever a child.

"We have to get started," Vy said.

"Huh?" Tree said lazily, reluctant to come back.

"Be time, Tree. We taking Dab on out."

"What?"

"Look, I ain't got the time now. Dab's so sick. You know it. It's my fault, dint want to face up to it. And you got the word from—but none of that could happen. It has, though. It has! My Brother! But Dab's got to go. He too sick to stay here."

"What you talkin bout?" Tree said. A chill came over her all of a sudden. She was suddenly really furious at M'Vy. She threw some kind of fit, and knew she was doing it. She couldn't stop herself because of the thought of Dab being taken away.

"To where!" she hollered. Taking him away got to her. Because they thought he was half-wit, they were going to take him out.

"Out where?" she yelled. "How I know where!" And threw the couch pillows up against the wall. She almost threw Warren Miller at the lamp, but then slammed it to the floor at her feet. "You ain't takin him *nowhere*." Spoken with dangerous calm.

"Tree," Vy said. But Tree turned away and wouldn't let Vy come near her.

Tree was big and growing bigger. Not as large as Vy, but she was strong and she could do damage, becoming wild when cornered.

"Who you?" Tree said, turning on Silversmith. "Coming in here like you king somebody. You not my father. I ain't got none."

"Oh, Lord, it my fault. Forgive her, Silversmith, forgive us, I'm to blame." Vy turned her face away.

Silversmith went to her and folded her close. Tree watched, seeing his ease with M'Vy, as though such feeling enveloped them all the time.

Because he care, Tree thought through her anger. Like I care for Dab. He love M'Vy, like I love a ghost.

The awful feeling drained from her. Tree sat down and soon was very still. She kept her eyes on her hands. "Dint mean to do it, M'Vy," softly she spoke. "Mr. Silversmith, I'm sorry." She was bewildered at herself, at her sudden swings of mood and heart. Slowly her anger went. She felt alone, which was how she was used to feeling. But now she knew she didn't want to be by herself with Dab anymore. It came to her that she did not *like* being alone with him.

"Everything gone be okay," Vy said soothingly. She sat next to Tree, hovering over her. "My honey, my Sweet Tree, you don't know what going on. I don't neither, not all of it." She sighed and looked around at Silversmith. He came over, sat down next to Tree and took her hand. Such gentleness seemed to be his way.

"Tree seen something," M'Vy said. "I kept from mentioning it you before because dint want to talk the subject on the phone. Tell you only that something happening here and to get on over quick, the boy be ill. But it was more," Vy said.

"My daughter, Tree, has seen the *mystery!*" And in a whisper, Vy went on, "Oh, when I was a girl, they talk about it. Long time, in a place deep in country. New Jersey, where I come from, before the whole lot of us family re-move to near Wilberforce. Back then, you wouldn't think there was some cities close by. New York. Because of so much country sky and thick country woods. In the hollows lived black folk. When it rained, the dirt roads ran to mud. They owned all that land of rain and mud and what roads they made. What I remember most was that, so far separated, there was nobody come pick up any trash, our garbage or our plain old junk the way they do now. We had mounds of wrecked things half-buried in the mud. Shoot. Talking bout land fill! We bury our garbage, feed it to animals, feed the flies.

"I never seen the *mystery*," Vy said, simply. "But I remember the talk. Like it happen this morning! Old womens, hanging around. They didn't belong to nobody no more, even they chilren had left the place or died off. There was one who'd look at me and say, 'Afrique! Afrique!' And say some kind of words that rolled out of her like dancing on drums. And she told of *mysteries*, the way you learn them and see and feel *them*. I guess my Tree doing something right. For she seen without nobody telling her how. Say it's in the blood of centuries, comin down the line, just like health or sickness. Dab seen it. It in him, too, down the line, blood and sickness!"

"Vy, what's this you're trying to tell me?" Silversmith said.

"I'm just so worried you won't believe it," Vy said. "But do believe it, for it's truth." She smiled apprehensively. "You know, I'm only a practical nurse. I had a year of training but not near enough to become an RN."

"Vy," he said, "what you do is worthwhile; no need you apologize."

Tree loved the way he caressed M'Vy with his eyes and voice.

"What I mean," Vy said, "you might not taken with ghost." She looked him straight in the eyes. "But there be a *ghost* here in this place. I know my Tree! This girl wouldn't lie about nothing. This girl, alone here with

130

her brother—and faithful to me! She been living with it until I come on back. I know this ghost to be my brother, yes." Vy said. "Tree, nor Dab, has never seen or heard of my brother."

"But why?" Silversmith asked. "Why not know you have a brother? You never told me." He looked pained, hurt.

"Because. Because. I dint have the heart—it's a long story. Or about they father, either. I lied about him. I kept it closed. You close a fist so you can beat the fate!"

"Vy, what is it? You have to make more sense than you making, hon." Without taking his hand from Tree's, he took Vy's shoulder and patted it gently.

He make it right, Tree thought.

"Well." Vy began again. "Tree taken me to the little room down the hall where she like to do things, be by herself. Draw things. That's where she seen it. Tree?"

Tree spoke promptly. She knew what Vy wanted her to say. Just the truth, as clearly as she could. It wasn't hard for her to talk about. It came easy, the way it stayed in her mind. "First time, I see him on the street," she said. "He standing by himself. He real good-looking, about eighteen. Then he come on up here, but I mean, he don't walk up here like anybody. He *appears* through the round table in the little room. Come, standing there the same way as in the street, all dressed to kill. Lookin cool. So beautiful dude, I swear he is! But he *through* the table, that's how and when I know he be a ghost."

"When Brother die," Vy said, "Brother be his name, we lay him out in a fine suit and shirt he have, like we lay out his brothers. . . . But he a man, then. Can't see why he visit Tree eighteen year old."

"Did he say anything to you?" Silversmith asked Tree.

"No sir," she said. "He holden something in his hand,

131

like a mirror. When I look in, I see springtime. Real pretty, freshening. I go in it." While she spoke, she was thinking about what Vy had said, about Brother having brothers, *we lay out his brothers*. His brothers die, too? Tree wondered.

"She taken me to the little room," Vy told him. "I didn't see. I felt him, though. It was Brother. My baby brother!" she stifled a sob. "So long time! He come visit my Tree. Some say the *mystery* come in a *seeing* light."

"It true!" Tree said. "I see the light and then him."

"That's how it was for Tree and Dab. I don't doubt it," M'Vy said. "I would give anything to see. But it not for me. Not now or ever."

"You believe in ghosts?" Tree asked Silversmith. She was too shy to look at him after her tantrum.

"Shoot," he said, and squeezed her hand. They were close, the three of them. "Folks stay with us, whether dead or alive," he said. "Ways to keep time from wearin out. I know a lady talk to her dead mama anytime she need to buy a new dress for her baby. Now a new dress mayn't be much to you and me, but for a poor woman alone, it takes some calculating. And she ask her mama what kind a dress and where to purchase. The mama right there in her place at the foot of the bed, too. Tell the lady where to go and how much to pay and never a cent more. Shoot. Ain't nothing to it. It just our way. Black folks is gifted."

M'Vy grunted, then giggled. Tree giggled. "How we gifted?" Tree said, laughing.

"Any way you name," Silversmith said. "We see what ain't there. We see through anybody."

"Shoot," said Vy. "But it the truth." Sobering. "Something, in health and sickness, down the line."

Tree stared at her. Gazing through her. "How come you never tell anything?" Tree said. "Where are Brother's brothers? No, where my *father*? How come you never tell anything. Why didn't I even ask until now? Was my father killed?"

"Killed?" said Silversmith. "*Killed*?"

"Listen," Vy said, "you don't know. No," she said to Tree.

"He was in the car when Brother die," Tree said.

"Who told you that!"

"M'Vy, I told you, you saw, we go in that place. He died in the crash, dint he, my daddy?"

Vy was shaking her head. "Brother die in the crash, yes, and it all my fault. Every bit of him was broken bones but he look just like he sleeping. Just one mark under his chin where they say the car door hit him.

"Oh, it my fault!" she continued. "My fault! But you daddy, Tree. He didn't have a scratch. That bike lady, him, walk away from the wreck, not even a broken fingernail."

"Then where he is?" Tree cried. "Where my dad?"

"Oh," Vy murmured, "oh. Oh." Her voice rose like a question. "Oh, that man. Your father and my brother did so love the Cincinnati Reds baseball and the night games!" Big tears streamed down her face. "Like two kids, couldn't wait to get there, sit in the bleachers. Never knew how much of a game they watch. It was being there they loved. They come back renewed."

"Where my father?" Tree said, as calmly as she could. "You got to tell me."

Vy smiled at her. Wiped her eyes absently. "Don't know," she said. "Been a long time now. Brother dying be one too many sorrows. He walk away one day. Came off the job but he never come back. Some say he went to Cincinnati, but I never knew. Didn't go looking. A woman, a mother of two kids, cain't just pick up and go hunting."

She held onto Silversmith's hand. Tree held tight, her mind stunned.

Got me a father, she thought. Find him and lose him in one day, too.

That didn't matter. Only one thing mattered to her. He alive!

CHAPTER

12

Things happened fast. First, M'Vy talking about Tree's father and baseball. And before that, talking to Silversmith, talking about Tree's father, talking about ghost to this man Tree never had seen, not until this day.

Talking about baseball and how her father loved it. Tree didn't know for certain one thing about him or what had become of him. Just that he was gone but not dead. She had let so much get by her.

How'd that happen? she wondered.

She didn't know a whole lot about other families. On TV, families talked together. They told things at the supper table or the breakfast table. They knew about all kinds of things going on in town, in the family—Grandpaw this and Grandmaw that. Roots.

How come I never think to ask anything? She answered her own question.

If you never told there's some answers, how you gone know the questions?

She never knew to ask about some father for the simple reason she had no idea there was one. Just a mention of him dead. And not even a picture, nor M'Vy ever mentioning him again.

All these years! They seemed suddenly to well up in Tree, like water rising to drown her.

Musta thought we some disgrace, me and Dab. If I

thought. If someone won't be there and nobody says, then you must think the worst about it. Is it? You don't think much on disgrace, either, she thought.

Within the confines of never having a father and no mother present for most of the time, she had carved out a narrow life for the two of them. Her and Dab. Them, in the rooms with Warren Miller. She, taking care of Dab and doing homework. Going to bed tired, with some amount of emptiness she allowed herself to realize. Getting by. She, knowing quiet for years, the way other children knew noise and lots of laughter. If she was ever terribly unhappy in the quiet, if she had missed something, she had known it only as absence. M'Vy. Until now.

Brother Rush be come, show me, she thought. A great swell of sadness came over her. Seeing some of Rush's world, she knew how empty was her own. Knowing she had a father like she had dreamed him made the loss of him all the more heartbreaking.

Why M'Vy keep him hidden. Why Rush, hidden. My dad! My dad! He and Brother love the Cincinnati Reds. Just like anybody, just good men. Why!

She didn't have time to find out. Silversmith had helped her off the couch. She didn't need help. But he was a gentleman; he gave a hand to ladies.

Like somebody I know for a long time. He do seem. Big, just like a father.

M'Vy, suddenly hurrying them. And Tree just then becoming aware of moaning that must have been going on for some time.

How I forget Dab? Talking to Silversmith like he somebody. First thing comes Dab, she thought firmly, then the rest. But maybe sometime, sometime, first one comes be *me*. Huh!

The next moment Silversmith and M'Vy and she were standing over Dab in his bedroom. Surrounding his bed.

Tree glanced at M'Vy to be sure the man, big Silver-smith, ought to be there.

M'Vy saying to Silversmith, "Give the boy something to ease him and it will mask the sickness. I'm gone have a time gettin it over. Why I waited. I dint wanta face the truth, no. I dint know, I wasn't sure, and that's the truth. I truly did not know until I get back way-time this morning."

"If it bad, you better to call Emergency," said Silver-smith. "They most able to handle something bad. Is it bad, Vy?"

She scrutinized Dab. Dab trembled, holding his stomach. Moaning, he looked like an old man.

M'Vy shook her head. "First thing, Emergency might give him something to handle him. Maybe anything could be the wrong thing."

"They don't give nothing lest a doctor tell them," Silversmith said.

"First thing they think they see a druggie and they call it in but they don't know what they callin. They thinkin withdrawal, but that not it, only. Oh, Lord. Lord."

M'Vy was speaking low, swiftly, to Silversmith. Silversmith, nodding and asking questions.

Tree leaned down to her brother. "Dab. Dab," she said. "It me, Tree. Teresa. Sweet. Dab. Dab."

His eyelashes fluttered opened. He didn't turn his head toward her. He had no strength for even small moves. "Huh," he grunted.

"It me," Tree told him. "I'm gone stay with you, bro. Everythang gone be all right."

This last brought a spark of strength to Dab. "Is it? Is it?" he murmured. He had a tiny, clear voice. It had country air to it, the way M'Vy's did, Tree thought. He turned his head slightly, grimacing. He managed a wan smile.

Tree leaned very close and kissed him tenderly on the

137

cheek. Never had she done that, that she could remember. His cheek felt on fire. His breath shook at her touch.

"It still hurt you?" she said.

"Uhhhhm," he moaned.

Tree didn't touch him again. M'Vy motioned to her and whispered to her. Tree leaned close to Dab's ear again. She told him, "There a man here, M'Vy's friend, Silversmith. Everybody call him that. He helpin us take you to—where we goin?" Tree asked M'Vy.

"Hospital," Vy said, hardly moving her lips.

Dab's eyes went wild. He had heard. Feverish strength seemed to fill his eyes. They swung back and forth from Vy to Tree. He vomited on himself. Down his bedclothes. M'Vy left the room and came right back with her coat and heels on, stuffing a folder of typed papers into her pocketbook. Then she ordered them.

"Tree, you standing here. You got three minutes. Get dressed. We gone."

She rushed to the bathroom and back with wet cloths and dry towels. She and Silversmith cleaned Dab up and changed his sleeping clothes.

"Nothin to it," Vy said, wiping Dab's face with a cool, damp cloth. She cleaned his neck where the vomit had run down. What Dab had brought up was mostly liquid. It had an odor, sweet and sour.

"Now you got but two and a half minutes," Vy told Tree.

"Oh!" Tree said. She left, and she was no more than two minutes getting dressed in her room. Long practice from being nearly late for school so often. She could take a quick shower in sixty seconds. Comb her hair, get in her clothes in another minute; and her shoes, in less than a half-minute. On her way back to Dab, she heard M'Vy call.

"Comin!" she called back. She took her purse from the table in the hall. Grabbed her raincoat from the closet. Carefully she avoided looking at the closed door of the little room farther down the hall. Then she couldn't help herself. She went to the door, listened. "Brother?" she whispered. She felt close to him now, closer than before. She wanted to open the door, to see if he had come to take her out again. But she thought of the distance between life and death, that she was in the distance, and she did not open the door.

It was time to go.

She went back to Dab, and they had him fixed up and ready to wrap him in a big old quilt Vy had produced. The quilt was yellow with flowers. Carefully Vy and Silversmith rolled Dab in it. And tenderly Silversmith lifted him in his arms.

Still, Dab cried out. He was weak; he couldn't yell too loud as they left the apartment house. The other tenants, some of them, must have heard the moaning passing their doors.

They went down dim halls and down three flights of stairs, avoiding the elevator. It was a safe building, with locked double doors, and only the tenants had keys. Tree always worried about being trapped with some stranger between the double doors. She knew that someday it would happen, with the outside door closed, locked behind her, and someone breathing down her neck while she unlocked the inside door.

This early evening the halls were empty. Tree could hear televisions. Laughter on the tube and news updates. Folks were home, finishing out the Sunday. Tree knew tenants to say hello but she did not get friendly. She did not want help, or people spying. She never had time for anybody else but Dab, anyway. She was glad she and M'Vy and Silversmith didn't encounter anyone on the stairs. Silversmith carried Dab like he was light as a feather. Dab's head was against his chest.

Like a baby, Tree thought.

Dab's eyes were closed. He would gasp in a sharp intake of breath. M'Vy eyed him anxiously, one hand now on Silversmith's shoulder.

"Dint know what you walking into," she said to Silversmith. "Bring you all this trouble."

"Don't mind some trouble," he said quietly. "Trouble is human. We bound to have it one time."

"Thank you much," softly, Vy spoke with feeling.

"Nothing to it," he said. "We gone get it done right."

They were outside the building, going down the steps.

Outside was night and dark clouds, wet and misty. This was Waltham Avenue, known for its complex of low-income housing, like the building Tree lived in.

"It not a bad place," M'Vy had once said about the city. "Got a good medical facility. I get jobs. Other medical centers all around. I get work. But you remember, Tree, when you grow up, don't take no half-measure. Get all the education you can think of."

Funny how you remember something when you not expecting any such thing, Tree thought. She had been filled with worry over Dab for so long, and suddenly there came M'Vy's voice about the city and about what Tree would have to do.

Don't think they give me a chance to grow up, she thought. Be this kid taking care of Dab all my life.

They stopped in front of a car parked at the curb. Tree knew at once that this was M'Vy's car. In the light of the street, it looked two-toned, black and darker.

"What color?" she said. "What color is it?"

"Black and gray," Vy told her, unlocking the door. "It got this line of maroon between the black and gray. You'll see when it's daylight. It real pretty.

"Put him down in the back," Vy said. "I'll ride with him. Lay him out," she told Silversmith. "Easy now." She moved the seat up so there would be more room for Silversmith to maneuver.

Silversmith was strong. Tree watched as he crouched with Dab in his arms and moved into the back and laid Dab out on the seat.

"Now come on out," Vy said. "You and Tree in the front. Me and the boy in back."

Tree felt the distance between M'Vy and Dab by M'Vy not calling him by name.

Wonder why she do that? Tree thought. Never like that with me. But I already know. She can't take it the way I do, like it be just Dab and the way he is. Telling you, when this over, we gone talk about some things, Tree thought.

M'Vy got in the back. She settled herself on the floor next to Dab's seat. Before, she had directed Silversmith to place a pillow back there under Dab's head. Tree knew that M'Vy hadn't touched Dab, her own son, herself.

Tree was also beside herself with excitement.

In a car!

It belonged to M'Vy, too, which meant it was almost Tree's car. Tree's family car. Her brother was sick, but she couldn't help being happy and excited about riding through the night for the very first time. Right next to Silversmith. He turned on the motor and the lights and some heat, for the air was chill and wet. He reached across and locked Tree's door. Adjusted the mirror and his seat so he was comfortable. Then they left. M'Vy guided the way.

"You know where Community is?" Vy asked him.

"Not sure how to get there from here," he said over his shoulder.

"Well, go on north and go on to Lane Avenue no more than six miles," Vy told him.

141

"Is that the way?" he said. "I know from Lane. That's the back way."

"Back way quickest," Vy said. "Called and say I'm bringing my son for admittance. They say, who is the doctor. I tell them it's the clinic, any doctor we can get." She laughed. "Tell them I'm a practical nurse and I got Blue Cross. They say they can give him a room if he need it."

Tree heard Dab gasp and moan. Then she heard sounds as if he were shivering. She didn't dare turn to look back there. She knew his eyes would be wide and scared. Dab was hurting and getting worse.

What can it be? she wondered.

Despite his hurting and also her fear of hospitals and what happened to people who went to hospitals, she couldn't keep her mind from the beauty of M'Vy's sleek new car. But the fear came back.

Say, you go in a hospital, you maybe not come out. Who say that? Tree thought.

She couldn't remember. Did Rush say that? Did I hear it through Rush's place?

She wasn't sure.

Old folks say, you go to hospital, you bound to die. Only take once.

She couldn't keep her mind on it. She felt the fear of it touch her heart and turn it to ice. It melted away, drying up like rainwater on a sunny porch.

When I grow up and have my own things, she thought.

The car smelled new all around her. Clean and new, like no other smell in the world. No other power was like this power motor in a good car. Good Chevy. Had to cost some money. Maybe Silversmith did help buy it.

"This part your car?" softly she said, for Silversmith alone to hear. She knew he was a nice man. He wouldn't

142

be angry at her asking. A girl her age might not have all her manners. He wouldn't get upset.

"I help your muh when I can," he told her. His voice, mixed in with sounds of driving, of gas surging. "We get this car for her," he said. "She got the title to it. This is Vy's own car."

"Huh!" Tree said with pleasure, and was silent again.

She let her hand glide on the cushion seat.

Feel like velvet! Tree felt as if she were in the safest place in the world.

When I'm sixteen. Driver's Ed. Get me the permit like all the kids do. M'Vy go driving wit me. Every evening fore it dark. Things be different by way then. It got to be different.

The thought of taking driving lessons was for Tree like discovering a sunken treasure. Right there inside her were things she'd never thought of, never knew she wanted. Slowly, now, she began uncovering them.

I buy the gas. I buy the gas for this car, for the times M'Vy let me take it over on weekends. Have me this job. Working waiting on people at places like . . . like . . . McDonald's! Or you work at the check-out in the supermarket. Well, you go get something pays more. More like, you go study. Work in a hospital. Never been to one. So I don't know what jobs they are. But I can find out. I can do it!

Silversmith drove fast down dark roads. Tree recognized Rinks, where they could get clothes at discount. That was where she got her raincoat. Then all was dark and country. She wondered how a hospital got to be way out in nowhere. There were fields and traffic lights at crossroads. They passed a large vocational training center.

Guess the country full of all kind of things, Tree thought.

They had been on Lane Avenue. They came to a traffic light and there was a blue-and-white sign with an *H* and an arrow pointing left. Silversmith turned the car left and they were on a four-lane, divided street. They went for a long time and there were houses, and more houses and lights.

Tree could see by the streetlights. Dots of rain covered the windshield. Silversmith turned a knob, and windshield wipers cleaned off the rain. When the wipers were turned off, the little dots appeared again.

It was so funny, all those little dots. Tree stifled a laugh. Through the window, she saw something looming out of pink mist of sky up ahead of them. Higher and higher it went up, like an enormous, layered wedding cake Tree had seen in a magazine.

"Hospital," Silversmith told her, pointing at the cake through the windshield of tiny dots.

"Is it?" Tree said.

"Yeah, a big medical center. Called Community. Real good, too. Vy will get on there one day."

"What you do for a living, Silversmith?" Tree said. But he was concentrating hard, trying to see over the slick black roads that washed out the car headlights.

"You got to go pass it," Vy was saying in back of them. "Round the corner past the emergency entrance."

"You sure you don't want to take him to Emergency first?" Silversmith asked.

"That won't be quicker," Vy said. "They back up sometimes for two, three hours."

"Okay," he said.

"See where it say General Admittance—Parking," she said.

"There it is," Tree said. "Right here. Here on my side."

"See it," he said and slowed, easing the car into the

144

parking area. "Carry him from here. Be just as quick. He don't weigh nothin."

"Hurry," said Vy. She was getting out of the car, as Silversmith parked it.

Tree could hear Dab. It sounded like he had some mess from a bad cold in his throat.

Hurry, get it over, she thought. Dead or alive, poor him. She felt tears coming. "Tired of cryin," she told herself, and held herself tight within.

CHAPTER
13

Silversmith carried Dab high in his arms.
Like Dab be some chocolate candy, Tree thought, and the slightest heat gone melt him.

M'Vy came in the lobby of the hospital at Silversmith's side. She looked too tall, too wide, Tree thought, in this unfamiliar place. Vy clutched her black suede pocketbook to her chest. It was as large as an overnight bag, it looked to Tree.

Swiftly Vy headed for a long counter with a sign suspended above it: Admittance.

They were some parade, Tree thought uneasily, coming on in order of importance. She was last, slouched low in her raincoat.

Wish I had me a scarf to cover my head, she thought. Her hair had started to frizz from the damp night outside.

I rode in a car, first time. Now I'm here, all in one same night. What come up next? Takin care of Dab is it.

Tree was scared, and tight as a drum inside.

Come in some double doors, nobody have to touch em to slide em open in front of you. They do that for everybody, she thought. And added up what had happened so far: You enter a large place where they're seats and people sittin, talkin and lookin like they waiting.

She put these observations in a safe place so she could tell Dab everything when he got well.

146

Off to the side, she saw a flower and gift shop. There were more counters with desks behind them. Signs: In-Patient, Out-Patient, Accounting, X-Ray.

An organized place, Tree summed up.

There were elevators forward from the waiting room. A wide hallway led from the waiting area to the area of elevators. She watched a guy dressed in white wheel somebody lying on a rolling bed inside one of the elevators. It was something, to see a bed fit in an elevator. But as the elevator doors closed, her heart sank.

Suppose they put Dab in a bed and take him away somewhere.

She sucked in her breath at the thought that Dab might die in an elevator between floors.

Don't dare to think it!

She heard M'Vy talking to the lady who had come up behind the counter. M'Vy smoothed her hand along the counter top. "Let me see the nurse," she said confidently.

Tree thought the lady was a nurse, for she wore a white uniform. Obviously M'Vy could tell she wasn't. Soon another woman in white came to the counter. She was older. "Can I help you?" she asked M'Vy. Pretty woman, she had on a name tag and a little pin on her lapel. Tree couldn't read the name tag from where she was standing.

M'Vy commenced talking close to the woman's face. Tree leaned around Silversmith to hear her. Talking, Vy pulled the folder from her pocketbook and planted it next to the nurse's hand. Tree guessed at the amount of control Vy was using, to not hurry and not raise her voice. Not to break down in tears.

Vy was saying that she was a practical nurse herself. She'd never worked in a hospital. But her group, while she was training, had taken a class in one. She'd seen things done, M'Vy explained.

"That my son," she said, turning toward Dab. "He

hurt and I call on ahead. You look, you find my name, Viola Pratt, bringing her son, Dabney Pratt. Look. The boy got some drugs and maybe he strung out a little bit, but he not a druggie."

She searched through her pocketbook and came up with a handful of envelopes with the pills and capsules in them that she and Tree had found hidden in Dab's room. She showed the envelopes and flashed a few bright capsules, but she didn't hand them over to the nurse. The envelopes disappeared inside her pocketbook as she talked on.

"But that just part of the problem with him," she said. "Another part is that Dabney some amount of retarded, you unnerstan? He just some slow. It worrisome, be slow. But that not so much. What it is be *this*." She tapped the folder and edged it toward the nurse. The woman took the folder. She kept her eyes on Vy until they shifted momentarily to Silversmith, still carrying his burden. They lingered a long moment over Dab, studying the illness that could be observed. Last, the nurse glanced at Tree, up and down; then, looked back at the folder.

"My boy is a *porphyric*," M'Vy said, emphasizing the unusual word. The nurse frowned slightly.

Her eyes were gray, Tree noticed. They were distant.

"You-all might not even heard of it," Vy said, not without pride, "for it most rare—*p-o-r-p-h-y-r-i-c*," she spelled. "You know, one havin the disease porphyria.

"Know yo'w like to have the doctors say they own cases," Vy rushed on. "I'm only tryin to explain what I alone happens to know. My boy is acute intermittent porphyria, or porphyria cutanea tarda, or symptomatic, they hard to classify. But they happens to them between ages seventeen and fifty." Vy spoke as though she had the words memorized. "Porphyria may be precipitated by alcohol or by drugs, but Dabney not no druggie—"

148

The nurse interrupted. "You need to have a doctor admit you, Mrs. Pratt."

"I know that. I know that," Vy said earnestly. "But Dabney havin stomach pains. He say it hurt him, too, all over. He say the light like to kill him, tellin me to find a faster way to let him die. You ever have to listen to a boy talkin like that? Will you please get him an internist?" Vy paused. Her voice was shaking. "Any of them look Dabney over, they'll see signs it's porphyria of some kind. He is constipated somethin awful. But there won't be a intestinal obstruction. That won't be it. His urine the color of Coca-Cola. My God, that's a dead giveaway — porphyria! Dangerous at this stage."

"We will leave the diagnosing to the specialist," the nurse said. She had read a minute from the folder. Now she closed it and held it against her. She wasn't being unkind. But she was crisp, like a cold head of lettuce. "Before we go any further," she said, "we have to make your son a chart and give him a name band. Mrs. Pratt, I want you to give the clerk all the information she asks for. Just go right there over by the typewriter. She'll take everything down for you."

"But Dab got to see a doctor!" Vy said.

"The sooner we get the forms filled out, the faster I can get him a cart and have him taken to his room," the woman said. She was quite firm.

M'Vy went back to the clerk. "How do you want to pay for this?" the clerk asked.

Vy took out her wallet. "I don't have company insurance because I don't have a company," she said. "I got some bitty insurance, but it so expensive . . . I wasn't expectin nothin like this." She took out a card, handed it over.

"I'll need your name and address, where you're employed, your son's name, date of birth," said the clerk.

"If you need it, we can get a social worker to help you work out the financing."

"Yes. Yes," Vy said. "Please. Please. Bring the nurse back here," she said urgently, and the clerk signaled for the nurse.

After a while, the nurse came. "Yes, Mrs. Pratt?" She still carried M'Vy's folder.

"The medical histories of my four brothers is in that folder," Vy told her. "You got in there, too, doctors' reports way, way back when of Willie, Chinnie, Challie Rush; and the last, my baby brother, Brother Rush. He the youngest."

"Mrs. Pratt, the sooner you get the forms—"

"—Brother my youngest *brother*. Brother his name, too."

There was despair in M'Vy's voice. Tree saw her face; it was anguished, scared.

"They all of them dead," Vy said, wringing her hands. "Chin, Challie, Willie and Brother. Brother die in a car accident but he had it, too. He try to hide it. Doctors couldn't save any of them. They were treated with barbiturate sedatives, you know. Barbiturates make them go crazy. And make the porphyria ten times worse. Barbiturates is *counter*productive. Your doctors better know that it can kill. That's why the boy took on so sudden."

"Mrs. Pratt, I'm not unfamiliar with porphyria. I have seen one or two cases. If you'll get half of the forms done, I can call the resident and see about a specialist."

"Please, yes," Vy said. "Don't let him die—me, standin here, explainin. Give the doctor the folder, oh, please." A shiver passed through Vy's body. She clamped her mouth shut, holding it in.

The clerk was busy with someone else. It took five minutes before she got back to Vy and began asking questions again.

Tree was right there, leaning around Silversmith, who still held Dab in his arms. She couldn't believe they'd make him wait like that, with a sick person in his arms. She had heard almost every word Vy said. Now she felt dazed. Her arms felt chilled.

What it is. What? Por . . . a disease. What it called? Dab has it. Will he die, like Brother die, and Willie . . . Do *I* have it?

Suddenly Tree was sick to her stomach. Her throat burned with a bad taste. She was afraid to breathe, so fear-sick was she all of a sudden.

In the next fifteen minutes, the clerk filled out more forms for M'Vy than Tree had ever seen. M'Vy signed her name to cards and forms nineteen times. Tree had counted. The nurse was on the phone with somebody. Then she was directing Silversmith to go with Dab someplace, Tree didn't hear all of it. But presently Silversmith was back and Dab was lying down on a kind of stretcher on wheels, like the rolling bed Tree had seen put on the elevator. Dab had a bracelet on that said his name. He was making noises, holding his stomach. He scrunched down; Tree knew he was trying to get out from under so much light. She had seen him do that before.

She wanted him to lie still. She begged him in her thoughts not to get so loud and make a spectacle and cause everybody to stare. She did want so to comfort Dab, her big brother. But he was so pale, he didn't look the same, and her heart was fluttering like crazy. So afraid she was to move and be seen by everybody.

I'll see you later, bro, she thought to Dab. See you in your room and we'll talk. Yeah.

She huddled close there behind M'Vy, watching Vy's hand move, signing and signing. She would never have suspected a hospital was so hard to get into. Vy was sweating down the sides of her face and down her neck clear

151

under her dressfront. Tree detected a faint odor of her sweat, and she knew M'Vy would be itching and feeling awful underneath her clothes. Tree saw the whole scene. Everything—the clerk, the nurse, other employees of the hospital, and all their jobs were a mystery to her.

Don't know nothing! Tree felt she would soon become nothing.

Finally all the forms, or most of them, were filled out. Dab was gone. Vaguely Tree had been aware of an orderly, a man in white, who had come up beside Dab's cart. But she had been distracted and wordlessly watched as her brother was taken away. Only Silversmith was there beside her. He went to Vy. She said something under her breath, not looking up from the forms. All this time Tree was having difficulty being out in the open, in the midst of the hospital. She felt exposed, hot and disheveled.

Why I feel ashamed? she wondered. Dab be sick, all it is.

She felt everyone looking at them; she stood out like a sore thumb.

Silversmith took her by the shoulder. He guided her over to the waiting area. She let him; there wasn't any reason to stop him. She would never have made it over there by herself.

"Your brother be all right," Silversmith told her. "Don't you worry, Tree. He is sick; I won't lie to you. But we get him some good help, and he'll be fine."

But it took too long, waiting, not knowing what was happening or where her brother was. Silversmith went back to the counter. The forms were taken away from Vy. She and Silversmith stood close together in the open area. They didn't seem to care that people all around would see them and stare at them—two big black people, looking out of the ordinary, looking *strange*, Tree thought, even if they were dressed nice.

Silversmith held M'Vy's upper arm. He looked around the room, serious, watchful and easy. He wasn't really seeing the room, Tree could tell. He was aware of comforting M'Vy and showing her that he was close with her.

Someday, Tree thought, I be like that. Stan anywhere and not care who lookin at me funny, or even twice. Can't see why I'm always so nervous somebody be lookin at me. So what? But it bother me a lot. Like, I can tell they not seeing *me*. They seeing what they think of me. You want to tell em where to go, too. Only time I feel okay, when Dab an me inside the house.

All at once, Tree felt something. Panicky, she looked all around. A feeling that the ghost was nearby. Rush. Out of the corner of her eye, she thought she saw something. When she looked, it was just a real person pausing before sitting down in a seat. People came into her line of vision; she would be startled. And would think of Brother Rush.

A woman in a white pantsuit came for M'Vy. Tree got up from her seat. Vy was moving away. Tree didn't know what to do, so she stood there, watching M'Vy enter an elevator and the door close on her. Silversmith was beside Tree. He had her by her elbows a moment. Man was always touching. Not in a bad way; it was nice of him. He made Tree less afraid.

"Where M'Vy go," Tree said as quietly as she could. "Where they taken Dab?"

"They took him where he'll be more comfortable," Silversmith said. "So they can give him the examinations. And Vy maybe can talk to some doctor about everything. I don't know how much they examine him already. Vy says all they have to do is give about two simple tests and they'll know it all. But whatever, it gone take some time."

"Where M'Vy, then?" Tree asked again.

"She with Dab, probably right there by his side, or soon will be," he said reassuringly. "They'll want to ask her some more answers. What going on ain't so common. But come on, Tree, I'll take you for something to eat."

"M'Vy say it be all right?" Tree asked him. "Shouldn't I stay close, case Dab need somethin?"

Silversmith looked at her kindly. It made Tree want to stay with him. "You won't be seein your brother for a while," he told her. "He have to be treated. But we'll go wait for Vy. She say for you to stick with me, okay?" He smiled at her. "You not afraid of me, are you?"

"No, me," Tree said. She looked right up at him. "If M'Vy not, I'm not either scared." He laughed, letting his voice boom. Tree glanced nervously around. People saw them.

Bet they think he my dad, too, she thought.

Some people even smiled when he laughed. "Follow me," he said. "I know a place right inside the building."

"What kind of place?" Tree asked. She came on reluctantly, still uncertain.

"A luscious place to eat, Tree; now come on." He took her by the hand over to the elevators. They got on one, and she looked at him all the way down. They went fast; her head felt light.

Once they were off the elevator, he told her they were below the ground floor. "There are basements even below this one," he said.

"How you know about this place?" she asked.

"Vy. But I knew they'd be a place somewhere." They turned a corner and before them was a place called Cafeteria and Coffee Shop. Tree could see inside through the glass front. There was a whole steam table, just like the cafeteria in her school.

"This place got a lot to offer," she said. "More than my

154

school cafeteria." She'd never seen such good-looking Jell-O, green and yellow and red and orange.

Silversmith took down two trays with silverware and napkins for both of them. Tree held onto her tray as they moved down the line.

"Get what you want," he told her.

"I don't know what I want," she said. "I don't eat so late in the night. But I like the looks of that Jell-O."

"Then have it," he said. "But there's cake and chocolate pie."

"You kiddin! Chocolate pie!" she whispered. She remembered M'Vy spooning thick chocolate sauce into a lightly baked pie shell. "Ummm!" she murmured, "I'll have the chocolate pie."

"I see some chicken down there," Silversmith said. "There's meat loaf and some mashed potatoes."

"You going to have some?" Tree asked him.

"I'll have me a little piece of meat loaf," he said.

"I'll have some chicken."

"You get some vegetables," he said.

Carefully Tree looked over the food. "Chicken and mashed potatoes. And some green beans," she told him. She could eat a bushel of green beans. "That will be all," she said as formally, as grown-up as she knew how.

"Well, you got to have some Coke to go with it." She nodded. "I'm going to have coffee," he added.

By the time he fixed a large Coke with lots of ice for her, her tray was full. Gingerly, she carried it to a table. They emptied their trays, and Silversmith took them away.

Tree was as excited as she could be. The food looked good. "It sure do smell nice," she told him, relaxing. Shyly she smiled at him as he sat down. "Thanks. I can pay you back." She couldn't resist taking two bites of pie. So tasty!

155

"I told you it was my treat, Tree." He looked at her like he cared a lot about her. She couldn't get over that.

The chicken tasted delicious. But halfway through her Coke, she thought of Dab. Sitting there, she let go of the straw and covered her eyes.

"What is it? What's wrong, Tree?" Silversmith said. "Don't you like the food?"

"Like it fine," she said. "I just tired, I guess." Watching her as closely as her own M'Vy would. He was like some mother. She didn't know what some father would be like. "The food tastin real good."

"Then what's the matter?"

"Oh, to eat . . . and you brother so sick, he can't eat nothin." She felt like crying. "It ain't fair. It just ain't fair."

"All so many chilren go hungry every day because they don't have *no* food," he said. "You gone stop eatin, too?" He didn't wait for an answer. "Because Dab is sick won't mean you got to be sick and not eat, too."

"But it ain't *fair!* I get to sit here and he can't even . . ." Tears filled her eyes.

"Come on now, Tree," he said, gently. "It never be wrong for you to eat when you hungry."

"Okay," she whispered. She wiped her eyes on her napkin. And took a deep breath, breathing in sadness, letting it out. She played with her food.

"Wish you'd eat, fore it get cold," Silversmith said.

She ate a portion of mashed potatoes to make him happy and sipped some Coke. But there were things on her mind. She had to ask him. "Why you suppose Brother Rush come to take me out?" she said.

It took him by surprise. He moved his coffee cup around on the saucer. "You need to think about some nourishment," he said, and laughed nervously.

"You don't believe it?" she said. "You don't think Brother Rush . . . maybe you don't believe in no ghost at all."

"No, I do believe you see what you say you see," he said. "I do. Don't ask me to explain why a ghost, and who see one. But I know some can and do. And you can."

"And Dab can," she said. "But why can't M'Vy see her own brother?"

"I don't know," he said.

"And why come Miss Pricherd see it? You know about Miss Pricherd?"

"I know," he said. "Did she see it?"

"Yes, but I pretend she seeing things cause she not eating right."

"Well, I don't know why you all see it," he said. "Maybe because the young is all innocence and the old is past innocence. But I don't know."

"You mean, not to be ashamed, innocence?" she asked. Here they were, talking so easily!

And he lookin just nice, and his clothes about perfect.

"It mean you can't harm somebody, innocence," Silversmith said. "You can't corrupt somebody. You free of sin. You ain't guilty of nothin. You free of guilt." His words rushed over her, cleansing her. "You got nothin to be ashamed of, Tree. You ain't hurt your brother. All you ever done for him is good. You ain't the cause of what's happening."

"But I am ashamed," she said, and bowed her head.

"Ashamed of what?"

"Just . . . of myself, sometimes," she said.

"You a pretty girl, unsure of yourself," he said.

Me, priddy? she thought. Me?

"You just self-conscious. It's nothing to be ashamed of. One day you become a full-grown woman. And the more you come to know, the more you will feel good inside about knowing."

"You ever feel ashamed about yourself?" she asked him.

"Not ashamed, Tree, just some self-consciousness as you growing up. You give it some space and it will pass on."

"Huh!" she said. She'd never guessed others could feel like she felt. "I thought I must be ashamed cause of my color."

He looked at her hard. Her face got hot, and she had to look away.

"Hear me, now," he said in his deep, soft voice.

Maybe he my real father! Ken! Tree thought suddenly. But that can't be. You know it can't. But whatever he was to her, Silversmith was caring.

"You can't separate your skin from what's inside it, Tree. Don't let nobody tell you otherwise," he said. "Your skin represent who you are. And how you feel about the skin is how you fare inside."

"But people look at you funny cause you dark-skinned," Tree said. Saying it made her feel better, less ashamed.

"People look at you all kinds of ways," he said. "Some look you over cause they don't like the dark. But that's their problem. And if the way they look at you make you change your feelins about yourself—make you feel bad inside—then you lettin *their* problem become *your* problem. You hurtin yourself."

"Yeah, that true!" Tree said.

"Sure it is," Silversmith said. "So how they lookin at you is *their* problem."

"*Their* problem," she repeated. "Yeah!"

"And don't always look to see how folks lookin at you. What you don't see, in this case, don't hurt you." He smiled at her, touched her hand.

158

She smiled back. When she ate again, the food was cold. But it was still good.

He don't seem to mind spendin the time wit me, she thought. Wonder if he ever read Warren Miller, somebody?

"You like to read some?" she asked him.

"Nope," he said. "I like the cable. Cable got everything you want to know. Vy and me do go to a movie once in a while. Mostly when she not too tired, we go dancin."

"Dancin! M'Vy, dancin?" Tree said.

"Sure! And not no disco stuff, either. Shoot. Vy likes the ballroom and big bands. Now that was a *time*. The fifties. She love it back then and the Latin numbers. Tito Puente's band. She loves the tango, and so do I. We'll take you with us one time, teach you a few steps," he said.

"Me?" Tree was astonished. "Dancin? Me?"

"Why not, you? You can dance, can't you? Vy will teach you, if you can't. My boy, Don, he can teach you. He nineteen. Catchin up in the Community College. He'll be all right. He likes computers. He takes the dances, mambo and tango and adds what he call a Brobeat to them." Silversmith smiled wryly to himself.

Tree didn't know what to say. She was overwhelmed by all the new things he was telling her. Dancin! Who'd think M'Vy be doin somethin like that?

And he was saying she could go dancing, too.

Guess his son, Don, will go dancin with the three of us. Tree thought about that and said after a time, "Guess you can be closed in someplace, but everything keep going on around you, don't it?"

"That's true," he said. "The world keep going; it have to."

"Nothin gone stop just because you's stop," she concluded.

They were talking about what concerned *her*. What

159

she cared about. Being with Silversmith was so nice. Being calm, grown-up, talking over food.

Tree looked up and saw M'Vy coming in. All at once she remembered Dab.

How'd I forget him like that! He'd slipped her mind completely. In just a short time, Dab had not existed.

A wave of guilt and shame rolled over her. She was terrified that her enjoyment would somehow do damage to her brother.

Silversmith got up, pulling a chair out for Vy, who sat down in silence. Tree wanted to know everything but couldn't bring herself to ask. M'Vy's face was shut, her eyes half-closed under heavy lids. She looked exhausted. Silversmith went to the counter and came back with soup and crackers, coffee and potato salad.

He know exactly what M'Vy want, Tree thought.

Vy drank her coffee, making slight whispering sounds as she sucked in the scalding heat. She held her coat closed with the other hand. She was big and honey brown. Vy was beautiful, Tree thought.

"They have to put Dab by himself," she said, setting down the cup. "He have to have a room kept dark. He most needs a high level of medical and nursing care."

Silversmith took Vy's hand, and Tree watched as they laced their fingers together. "He can't have visitors," Vy said. Looking at Tree, "I'll have to stay the night. Yo'w go on home."

Dab always wit me in the night. Tree was seized with panic. Never in my life be all alone!

"I'll wait in the house for you, Vy," Silversmith said, "keep Tree company."

Tree sighed in relief.

"And I'll call you later," Vy said. "Don't know yet when you pick me up."

"Okay," he said. "I'll sleep on the couch."

160

"You can use Dab's bed," Vy said. Tree looked at her sharply but said nothing.

"I'll just watch some television," he said.

"I'll be away from work for a few days," Vy went on. "What we can do—you bring over the car to here when I call. I'll take you to work and you tell them I won't be there for a few days. That's the way it will be. I got to stay here."

Tree looked from one to the other. "You both workin someplace?" she said. "Together?"

"Tree, there be much, but not now," Vy said. "You have to wait."

"I'm always waitin for *not now*, seems like," Tree said, gazing at her hands.

"Watch you mouth, Tree," Vy told her. Tree knew that she must let M'Vy do the thinking and worrying.

But awhile ago, he treat me like I'm a person.

She felt miserable and slid down in her seat, making herself smaller. Something sad and bittersweet commenced running through her head.

"Everything going to be okay," Silversmith said soothingly. But Tree didn't smile at him. She didn't pretend to agree with him.

I don't think it's gone be okay, she thought. I sure don't. It was strange not having Dab with her, like she had lost some part of herself.

They got up. Vy kissed Tree on the cheek, patted her shoulder. And yet her usual warmth seemed to be missing. Vy went out, and Tree and Silversmith headed home.

All the way there, Tree was distracted. She did not think to enjoy her second ride in M'Vy's car. There was this sound, which had once been a really good sound, running through her mind. She couldn't make it stop; and now it was scaring her to death.

She imagined Dab coming toward her in his shuffling light shoes. His voice was just as clear in her head.

Do a little dance, she heard him. *Sing a little song*, mournful, painful, *Do a little dance*, over and over again.

CHAPTER

14

Tree and Dab walked along. They were tiny figures against an enormous suspension bridge. They walked, one behind the other with Dab in the lead. Although it was night, Tree could see Dab's yellow shirt and his arms, held away from him for balance. She reached up and placed her hands on his shoulders. "You my big brother," she told him.

"Yeah. Yeah," he said.

"I'll always look after you," she said.

"You my best fren," he called back.

"You be dancin?" she asked him.

"Oh, yeah," he said, and he did a little dance in his shuffling shoes.

Tree was happy. Dab seemed more content than ever before.

The bridge gleamed under her feet. It was immense, looming above them. But then they weren't walking on the bridge. They were climbing a huge, thirty-six-inch cable. They were heading for a gigantic masonry tower that supported a whole span of cables. Through the tower windows, she saw sick people resting in beds. They were staring out.

The cable narrowed and became damp and slick. Tree slipped, sliding backward.

"Dab!" she cried.

But he didn't hear her. He was dancing up the cable; his shuffling light shoes showed him the way.

Tree couldn't hold on. She fell; falling, long and deep in the dark. She screamed for her brother, but he was beyond her, a dancing fool. Soon she would be gone. Still, she clawed at the night. She hit. She was lying dripping on a pavement. It was a wet highway. Cars flashed by. They had their lights on inside. She could see plush upholstery. She lay, wet and dripping as cars flew by. Her bones were dripping her flesh.

Tree woke up screaming and crying. Someone had hold of her and was lifting her back in bed, for she had fallen out. Someone patted her until she calmed down, and straightened her bedding. She knew it must be Silversmith who had taken care of her. But she dreamed it was sweet Dabney. Too sleepy to thank who it was. She felt ashamed at dreaming so hard and falling on the floor. Now she slept a sound sleep for the rest of the night.

Tree finally awoke to a house of silence. She lay a long time just listening. Nothing in particular. She heard her alarm clock on the dresser. She didn't even bother to look at it. She knew by the complete silence of the building that it was long past time for school or for work. The night came back to her as it had happened. Even the nightmare. She remembered the bridge and falling off the scary span.

She thought of Dab, closed her eyes tightly. She hugged her pillow until some of the sad feeling passed.

It me fallin down, not Dabney, she thought. Maybe him climbing and climbing and not falling was a sign he would be all right. Presently she felt better and swung her legs over the side of the bed.

The house was quite empty, she was sure of it. But she pulled on her blue robe anyway and walked to the door.

"Silversmith?" she called down the hall. She went to

the living room. Not a soul; but she saw signs that he had straightened up the room. She tried to find some change in the room, since only awhile ago it had held so big a man. But it wasn't changed.

Why it feel different, then? she wondered. No, it's me, she concluded. Me, changing.

She looked at the closed door of her little room.

Ghost, don't come now—me, by myself!

And hurried to the kitchen. There was a note pasted on the refrig. She sat down at the table to read it. And smiled. Silversmith wrote large. "LOOK INSIDE," she read. She got up again, stifling a giggle. It didn't seem right to be silly without Dab.

On a sudden impulse, she hurried to Dab's room. She opened the door and peeked in. His bed was still rumpled, the way they had left it. His pillow was on the floor. Dirty pajamas on the floor. Tree gathered up everything, including his trousers where he'd stepped out of them. She tried to figure out how long ago he *had* stepped out of them, but couldn't.

Just when she was about to leave, she spied something sticking out from under the bed. Part of a shoe was what it was. Tree smiled in recognition.

Dab's light shoes! she went over and got them. Held them, looked at them and slipped them on. She had to push her toes forward to make the shoes light up. They lit up, and she laughed. The next minute she was sobbing. Looking down at the shining shoes, she got hold of herself and wiped her eyes.

Oh, Dab! She walked to the bathroom, depositing the dirty clothes in the hamper, watching her feet. And went back to the kitchen, still watching her feet light the way ahead of her.

She sat down to read the note again. "LOOK INSIDE." She went over and opened the refrigerator. Two stacks of pint cartons were before her. There was another note

165

taped to them. "THIS IS WHAT'S LEFT, CASE I CAN'T GET BACK FOR YOUR DINNER. NOW LOOK IN THE OVEN."

"What?" Tree said out loud. "You some kind of crazy, Silversmith?" But the note made it a game. It was like Silversmith was there with her.

The oven dial was on on the stove. She peeked in the oven and found serving dishes of Chinese food. Tree *loved* Chinese.

Maybe he *is* my dad! She clapped her hands and laughed down at the shoes. "Look what Silversmith left us!" Talking like that to the shoes was almost like having Dab as close as could be.

The clock on the oven read twelve o'clock.

Noon! I never sleep that long even on the weekend, she thought.

With pot holders, she carefully took the dishes from the oven. Four dishes, different kinds. One was Chinese spare-ribs. Another looked like chicken and pea pods. There were noodles in one dish and shrimp in the other.

I can't eat all this!

She set her place at the table and, eagerly, she ate. And ate.

Um-um-uuum! Looking down at her light shoes, pushing her toes forward. "It's hot and it's good, real good. You'd love it," as though Dab could hear her. Tree hoped there was some way he knew she was thinking of him. "I have to eat," she said quietly. "But you still stay on my mind, every single minute. Everythang gone be all right." She held onto this thought. She would not let any doubt come near.

Tree spent the day by herself. There were things to do. She knew the routine. But before she could straighten Dab's room and change his sour-smelling bed, making sure everything was clean and neat, she had to know for certain about the little room—her round table.

After eating, she rested at the table in silence; it was more than an hour later. She left the dishes and went slowly down the hall. Halfway, she stopped and studied the shuffling shoes.

You ain't scared, are you? she thought to them. It was awfully quiet around her. She made the lights go off and on by moving her toes back and up. Nothing to be scared of, she thought. You with me.

"Ohh, wait," Tree said. "I forgot to call the school!" She always called when she or Dab was under the weather.

In the kitchen again, she called the school office. She told them Dab was ill in the hospital and that she wouldn't be in because she had the flu herself. Dab had pneumonia, she said. She didn't much mind lying over the phone. The aides weren't going to believe half of what she told them, anyhow. Over the phone they were just voices, and she was only a voice to them.

Be workin they jobs, she thought as she hung up the phone. Ain't got no time to care about me.

Dab got pneumonia and I got the flu, that's all it is. She headed down the hall again. She didn't stop this time. She came to the door and did not hesitate to open it.

She wanted to see Brother Rush now. She wanted him to take her out again. Yet, there was another part of her that was always very much afraid of seeing a ghost. But in the room now there was no mystery of strange light. There was no ghost through the table. She leaned on the table, reaching out over it. And passed her arm back and forth; closed her eyes. Rush was not settling in.

"You come on, take me out," she whispered. "I got on Dab's shoes. See? We got a lot of trouble. Dab sick like you was sick. Please come and tell me what gone happen to him."

But nothing came. She stood, arms outstretched, for five, ten minutes. And nothing settled in.

Bet I'd have to come back every half-hour to catch

him. Rush so fast! she thought. She remembered the times she had gone to the place of Rush and riding in his automobile.

Why I love cars so much, it came to her in a flash.

Staring at the table, she saw scenes of the past in her mind. She caught and held the one of the car crash, when she had escaped through the trunk. When Ken, her father, had lived and Brother had died. Thoughts snagged on the way Rush fell from the car.

What it is. Something. Seem funny.

She couldn't tell what was funny about it. Everything surrounding that moment was too much for her to fathom. To fall from a crashing car was the worst thing she could think of.

To fall. Falling. Fall from a bridge!

She was suddenly overwhelmed by a sense of closeness to death, and to Rush.

Brother got hit by that door. He got knocked cold, you could see it. To die, never knowing it happen. Never know how it feel when you hit the ground.

She turned and left the room, closing the door firmly behind her.

I got things to do. She took a shower, and afterward, when she was dressed again, she took away the dirty towels and put clean ones on the racks. Then she went about cleaning up Dab's room. It had an odor, so she opened the windows. She kept her mind away from all trouble while changing the bedding. She worked hard, so as not to think. She loved hard work.

Get me a job, do what I want to.

At three o'clock, the phone rang. Tree dropped the dust cloth and covered her ears, shaking all over.

Don't answer it. Answer it!

She ran to the kitchen and picked up the phone. "Tree," said the phone. It took her a moment to recognize the voice, her heart was beating so loud. It was M'Vy.

"Hi! M'Vy, Hi!"

"Hi, baby. How you doin? You all right? You find the food?"

"Yeah, I'm fine. The food was great. Silversmith bring it for me, keep it warm, too. He nice, M'Vy. I'm fine. What's happening? Where are you?" She didn't want to ask. She would not dare ask about Dab. Let M'Vy tell her all she wanted to. But she could not bring herself to ask.

"I'm at the hospital," Vy said.

"You ain't slept or nothing?" Tree said, her mind and heart racing.

"Oh, I slept a little. They give me a cot right with him." She avoided saying Dab's name, Tree could tell. "He still very sick, Tree. I did sleep. Silversmith brang me some change of clothes from where I live in."

"Oh," Tree said. "I . . . I don't guess he ask for me."

"He can't ask for nobody, yet," Vy said. "Listen, I got to go. You call the school? That's important."

"Yeah, but I only remember to about one o'clock. M'Vy, I slept clear to noon."

"Well, you were up so late, all that happened." She was silent, and Tree waited. "Listen, baby, I went out for lunch and now I'm in the hospital lobby. Dab got through the night, Tree; we thankful for that."

He got through the night! She commenced trembling. He got through, he didn't fall! It was me that fall from . . .

"Listen," M'Vy said, "I got to go. Silversmith comin over after he work and get cleaned up. He'll stop by here; maybe I can come home awhile with him; I don't know yet."

169

She soundin down, Tree thought. But she wouldn't ask how really bad Dab was.

"You might just as well stay to home in the morning," M'Vy was saying, "look after the house. Don't want folks knowing we all gone from home. Go back on Wednesday, all right?"

"All right," Tree said.

"What a matter, you?" Vy said. "Tree, don't go lonesome on me. Hold on, hon. We got to be strong . . . in our prayers for him," M'Vy finished.

"I know," Tree said, and whimpered. She couldn't remember when she'd prayed. She cupped her hand tightly over her mouth to keep from crying.

Vy sighed, "God help him! 'His eye is on the sparra and I know He watches me.'" The religion Vy kept lived in her favorite religious songs.

What it mean, on the sparra? Tree wondered. Why the *sparra* and *me?*

"Yea, Tree, you unnerstan me?"

"Yea, M'Vy," she lied.

"Yea, you prayin for your brother?"

"Yea, M'Vy!"

"Yea, Lawd." Vy hummed. "Bless this house. So it be all right."

"Yea!" was Tree's heartfelt response.

"Pray, everythang be good."

"Yea, everythang is good." Tears fell down her cheeks.

"Don't cry, my baby, don't cry. I got to go. Bless you. Be talkin to you; you know I love you, honey, Heart. Maybe see you later. Silversmith be comin after while, for company. Take care. Everthang gone be okay."

Vy hung up. But it wouldn't be okay.

Dab would live one day more.

CHAPTER

15

"Dab ain't gone no more funerals! He didn't die, he didn't die. No, he *didn't*, he didn't *die!* M'Vy, we prayed and everythang, din we? He *didn't*. You said . . . You said it be all right! He didn't, n don tell me he did! He didn't, no-he-din. He din. He *didn't die!*"

Tree ran through every room of the house, including her own little room of privacy with the round table, in which Rush would appear and disappear. She ran through Dab's room, which she had cleaned and disinfected and changed all of the bedding in, until it was as perfect as she imagined was the hospital room where he was getting well. She had bought a bunch of dried flowers for his dresser. She had painted a sign with poster paints and tacked it to his wall: WELCOME HOME, DABNEY PRATT, MY BROTHER!

But the moment M'Vy came through the door Tuesday afternoon, Tree knew the truth. Vy's face was swollen, discolored from grief. She had aged overnight. Silversmith supported her weight. She had caved in on herself, as though all her substance were gone.

Staggering, Silversmith propelled her into a kitchen chair. At once, Vy commenced talking and did not stop, even when Tree raced in and out of the room.

Tree could hear Vy's voice from anywhere in the house. There was no way to escape it, and she could not stop running.

"Tree. He gone, baby. You brother, he dead, hon, they couldn't save him. Oh, I'm so sorry. I'm so sorry. Yea, just after eleven. I was right there. I wouldn't leave him. Thank the Lawd I didn't. They did everythang they could—commere, baby, don't run like that. But it was too late. Oh, God. Once the respiratory paralysis start . . . You got to stop it before it begin. Prevent it. They have the respirator there, but it was too late. The cranial nerves, you see. God, it's my fault! I should've realized long ago. But you get so weary! So busy! Knew it long time ago. Yea, Lawd, he a boy, weren't he? I just wouldn't face it. The boys, mens in my family. But it's not something sex-linked. Found that out years later, after Willie. It can happen to a girl, a woman, but it didn't. Binnie die of one too many strokes. Shoulda had you both tested. But to do that, it seem like tempting fate. Who can face they children may die!

"Tree, that's why you got to go get the tests. Me, too. But he dead. Ain't it a shame! Shame! Maybe it for the best. The poor, sad boy. He couldn't think. What Dab gone do in his life, the way he was?"

Tree went crazy. Screaming at M'Vy, she was outraged, insane with fury. She shook violently. Her eyes were dry and sticking, raging. She ran around M'Vy, around the kitchen table, bouncing off the refrigerator. She felt no pain as she hit the corner of the stove hard. She thought of turning on the burners and putting her hands in the flames to get them warm, but she hadn't the time. She had to keep going. Her legs just went; she didn't have to tell them to or look down at them. They were on their own.

Silversmith tried to catch her and hold her. M'Vy spoke to him. "Let her alone," Tree heard her say. "Just see she don't hurt herself," she said. "Let her get it out of her system."

Tree hated M'Vy. She said so, over and over. And if she stopped moving, she would take a kitchen knife and put it through M'Vy, or herself, she didn't care which. Or beat M'Vy over the head until she lay still and breathless on the floor. Or plunge the knife in her own belly and fall down and let herself bleed out the hate and the love.

Tree saw the unreal in her mind and the real in the kitchen quite vividly. She could hear the sound of her own voice, talking and raging.

"Shoot! *Shoot! Damn* you, it your fault! *You* did it. You beat him. You beat him up. He didn't die; you killed him, M'Vy! He ain't dead, he ain't dead, unh-uh. My brother, Dab. He didn't, no he *didn't*, it's a lie! How come you didn't do something sooner? You don't even think of Dab, when all the mens die off. You killing him, can't you do something?"

One minute, she knew Dab had died; she had to believe it. The next minute, Tree would accept no such thing. And smacked her open palms hard against every object in the kitchen that couldn't smack back. She ignored Silversmith completely. She knew if she ever wanted to hurt him, she would want to kill him. Her hate for M'Vy was all-consuming. But rather than attack her, she would will the witch out of existence. In an instant, M'Vy was nothing.

"Tree. Tree," Vy said. She didn't try to touch her daughter. "I was so afraid. I was young. I didn't have no smarts—who did, back then? I beat that boy. I beat him, help me, I beat him. You won't forgive me. But I won't forgive myself. Maybe I thought if I beat him, people would think *he* really bad, blame him, not me." Vy covered her face with her hands. "But really all the time I was afraid he might have the sickness, like my brothers. I was so afraid, Tree."

"Afraid. Afraid," Tree said. Her voice was so calm and reasonable. "You, afraid? Big you and tiny him. He was really tiny. Stunted tiny and skinny legs. You beat him tiny. Brother Rush show me you and Dab way back then. You own brother, come to show me. You kill Dab. You kill him. You can never lie and say you cared."

"No, Tree. You can hate me, but I didn't kill him. He survived my worst." Vy moaned into her hands and cried.

"That Ken didn't know a thing," Tree said. "That Ken, just walkin away from me and Dab."

"Oh, Tree! You father was . . . troubled. I was young; I wanted everythang I see. Ken work from way morning to way night. But sometimes he go an gamble it up. Didn't matter to me when he won. It was that he left me alone; and me so young. I took it out on Dab."

Through it all, Silversmith stood in his very neat and clean business suit. He had on a handsome brown raincoat, belted. He was still within himself, until he spoke to Tree.

"You won't be bringing you brother back, callin down your muh and dad," he said.

"Yeah? Yeah?" Softly Tree answered him. "You quick to take her side. All you grown-ups stick together, huh? Talkin bout how *bad* be teenagers."

"That's not it, Tree," Silversmith said. "Vy know exactly what she done. What I have to say about it, I will say to *her*."

"That leaves me by myself, agin, don't it?" Tree said. She sucked in her breath and let it out strong. "I can say what I think. I can do that. How come he die so fast, M'Vy? How could it happen! How come he don't call on me!"

"Oh, hon, Dab couldn't think of nothin but the pain."

174

"Pain? All over him, pain? Oh, no. Oh, poor Dab. Poor, sweet Dab."

Vy got up with difficulty. "Tree, baby." She walked near, leaning on the table for support, but Tree wouldn't stay still. Vy had to move out of the way as Tree flung herself out of the room and down the hall.

She yanked opened the door to the little room. Plunged inside, slamming the door behind her. Rush was not there.

"He comin. I know he is. He been here, he comin again, you wait. Then, I'm gone wit him. I ain't comin back!"

Tree ran to the living room, climbing up on the furniture. She had to touch every piece of furniture and smack every wall. She found the Warren Miller book, and she did not hesitate. She flung it at the window. She heard glass crack. The book fell to the floor. "Yeah. 'The Time I Got Lost' in the ferny woods—good-bye, Dab, no more readin. Dab love that book. And it couldn't do nothin. Everybody let him go. God let him go. Nobody care but me, and I couldn't see him. Nobody even thought to takin his sister to see him. Be there, bet he wouldn't die. He would see me, say, 'Do a little dance, Tree.' I would have, too, if they give me the chance. But nobody care. Dab, what we gone do?"

Tree flung and hurled herself. She ran and ran until her feet were numb. Air would not stay inside her lungs. Her legs ceased to move, finally. She stood in the hall, sagging against thin air like a junkie flying high.

When Silversmith took hold of her, she was too weak to resist. He picked her up, carried her to her room and sat her against two pillows. M'Vy came in; sat beside her. Silversmith was on her other side. She was between the too big grown-ups, looking up into their faces. Had they ever been young? Each of them held one of her hands.

175

Her hands were without strength, clasped tightly in theirs.

The three of them sat there. Tree was panting. Cold sweat had soaked her neck and under her arms. She felt icy cold when she could feel beyond hoplessness. Her eyes closed and she was instantly asleep, unconscious. A few minutes later, she awoke, shaking the bed. Silversmith and M'Vy did not let her go.

"I got to go to the bathroom," she told them, and they released her.

"I'll go with you, help you along," Vy said.

"No. No," she murmured. "I can make it. I don't need you."

"She gone to the little room," she heard Silversmith say. It was in her mind, but she knew she had heard him.

"Let her go," M'Vy said back. Tree paid them no attention. She went to the bathroom and on to the little room. She went inside. Still, Rush was not there.

"Whyn't you come? Take me for a ride?" No sound anywhere. Tree lifted her hands over the table, reached into space there, but there was nothing.

"I'll come back," she told the empty room. "Every half-hour, I'll be here."

Later, M'Vy fixed her chicken soup. Tree swallowed a tablespoonful, but she would not take more. To take that much made her stomach turn. She breathed in heaving gasps suddenly as she fought down sickness.

"He really dead, then?" she asked, after a time.

"Yes," M'Vy said.

"M'Vy, y'all too close, I can't breathe." Vy slid from the bed and sat in the chair.

"Get on off my bed, Silversmith," Tree said. She didn't look at him.

He got up, but stood near.

"Standin makin me nervous," she told him. "Whyn't you go on out."

"Tree," M'Vy cautioned.

"Well, he don't have to be here in my room," Tree said peevishly. "It *my* room. Not used to having some men standin around in it."

"You can turn me out, Tree," he said. "I'm still gone like you."

Tree felt her mouth pull down, felt an awful sadness climb up her insides. "I like you, too," she said softly. "I don't want you in here. Please. I don't want nobody in here wit me if I can't have Dab."

"Tree."

"Please."

"Try to sleep," Vy said. "We can talk later. Do you have to go to the little room?"

"Yes," Tree said.

"The spirit world not for us to mess with," Vy said.

"Leave me alone."

"If that's what you want, baby."

"I don't want to talk to you no more. What they gone do with Dab?"

"They take care of . . . the body," Vy said bluntly. "It being taken care of."

Tree turned her face away. M'Vy went to the door and out, not looking back. Tree closed her eyes and fell asleep on all memory. Soon she was awake again, dragging herself out of bed and down the hall. "It time," she whispered. Been more'n an hour, I bet.

Silversmith and M'Vy were in the kitchen. Tree could smell fresh coffee. That's good. Leave me alone. Can't stand either one of them, she thought. She went inside the little room. Rush was just settling in.

I knew it!

The room filled with unnatural energy, energy that

was scattered but was pulling in around her. She knew the feeling. It entered her mind, where her thoughts were shaken up and rearranged in preparation for that which was beyond her knowledge.

She closed the door behind her and at once was with the gathering supernatural. She went to the table, raised her hands and stretched her arms out. Rush was settling in, capturing her in his mystery of unearthly light.

Rush was there.

"Uncle Brother, it me!" Tree whispered. "How you doin?" She grew shy. "I knew you my uncle, but sometimes I forgot and think you could be my boyfriend, you come here so young. Know you M'Vy's baby brother. I'm ready to go wit you."

Standing there, Brother Rush was perfection. Young and handsome, no sickness, he was dressed in his finest, as always.

Suit never get wrinkled! she marveled. Cause it made so fine. And that shirt!

Tree couldn't get over how sparkling the ivory-color shirt was. She looked him over carefully. Saw his silver belt buckle, *Jazz*, and his socks and splendid shoes.

Wish I could hear him play the piano, she thought. But not now; not the time.

She reached out for Brother, smiling. She did so love having him take her out.

And she was there.

Going for a ride! She was in the backseat of Brother's car, smelling odors of alcohol and cigars. She was the age she was in real life.

That's funny. I ain't a kid again?

But she didn't mind. And, as was possible in the ghost time, she was outside the car looking in through the windshield, as though she were the sunlight and shade of the countryside through which Brother was driving.

178

In the car next to him was Dab.

Well, no kiddin! Dab? Dab! It you! How come you here? you lookin *good!* How you feelin, bro? Dab, look at that suit!

Dabney Pratt had on a gorgeous suit. It had a pinstripe, but the background was gray instead of black or dark blue, like Brother's. Dab had on a bow tie; his shirtfront had pearl buttons.

That's nice! Tree said. Dab, you lookin as good as Brother. Where we goin?

It came to her where they would have to go.

The two of them, Brother and Dab. Brother was driving fast. Their faces were full in the sunlight. They were talking and laughing, having a good time. The sunshine on their skin didn't seem to bother them at all.

I'm so glad. Where you goin?

But she knew.

That's good, she said. Good, you get to go together. Maybe that the reason you come back to visit, Brother. Huh! Come to keep my Dab company.

Tree knew she must leave now.

Dreamin won't be the same as the for real, she thought.

In her dreams, she'd fallen off a bridge but Dab had continued up the span.

It didn't mean I fell and died. It mean that Dab went all the way up, the way you do *after* you die. I fell off to live; Dab stay on the bridge to God.

This didn't seem odd or silly to her at all in Rush's place, in the backseat of his car. M'Vy was not in the car with her. No one was in the back with her. Sunlight fell on her legs, and it was warm.

But Brother now turned around to look at her. He looked her in the eyes. Never had he done that before; but then, she'd never been in the car at the age she was in real life. Did that matter? His face was a dead man's face. It frightened her.

You scarin me. Turn back, she told the dead face.

Brother wouldn't turn around until she understood he was trying to tell her something. Again, she recalled the time he fell out of the car, with Ken, the driver. Only he didn't fall.

He didn't *fall. That's* what was funny. He didn't tell Ken about the girl in front of him. That split second might've made the difference.

Oh . . . Oh . . .

Brother's face was turned clear around. It was no longer a face; it was a skull, old and white. Roots of things began growing in it.

Let me out! Oh, I want to look at Dab one more time. No! Dab, don't turn around. Let me out! I got to go . . . I got to fall . . .

Tree was swooshing through the backseat of the car, through the trunk of the car. She was swooshing out as only she could out of Rush's place and time. She was falling. It was unpleasant. She held her breath through the supernatural.

Back to the room that was her little room, blinking her eyes, rapidly. Rush had come back with her. He was young again and looked so handsome. Through the table, he was big as life. He was in his mysterious light, dressed so fine.

"You lookin beautiful, Uncle Brother," she told him. She was calm. "Thanks for getting me home." She didn't doubt he saw to it she got back. "I wanted to see M'Vy so young. I want to be little so's I can play with tiny Dab one last time."

Brother Rush never said a word.

"Uncle Brother, thanks for the ride. But what you want wit me in the first place?"

180

Brother faded before her eyes.

"Wait!"

His light faded, taking Brother far beyond. Rush was gone.

You won't be comin back, will you? Tree didn't bother to ask.

She left the little room, knowing Dab was dead for good. Death was what he had now, what he had wanted. She knew Brother had not just fallen from the car. He might have even opened the door. Brother had *leaned* out.

That's somethin for M'Vy. But it don't change a thing. Just make Brother die sooner.

CHAPTER
16

"You brother *jumped*, M'Vy," Tree said. She came in the kitchen. M'Vy and Silversmith were eating stew in bowls and drinking hot coffee. Vy must have made the stew while Tree was upset and sleeping off and on in her room.

"What time it is?" Tree said, and glanced at the clock. "Five thirty! I been out of it all day." She talked calmly, but her pain was gnawing, deep. She was not certain how she would get through the night.

They were staring at her.

"I seen Rush, M'Vy," Tree said. Vy's face seemed to turn darker. Tree knew she was forcing herself not to look over her shoulder.

"He gone now; don't be scared," Tree said. "Gone for good, probably. I don't know. I ask him a last question, but he won't say. Knew the answer, anyhow. You brother didn't just get killed in a car accident. Ken didn't cause him killed. Brother Rush commit suicide. Least, he meant to."

Tears filled Vy's eyes, glistening like beads. "Don't, Tree. Oh, I know you hate me. But don't make no fun of my dead Brother!"

"M'Vy, I ain't makin fun. I don't hate you. I know, things I said. But Dab is gone—you know how long he's gone for? The whole rest of his life and my life, too. I

182

been cryin for me bein by myself, too. Dab and I . . . Dab and I . . ." Tree could not finish. She had no words to describe how alone together they had been. How she loved her brother!

She shook her head. "Don't know yet how'm I gone get through it. Don't know if I will ever get over it.

"M'Vy, I saw Dab in the car with Brother," Tree said. "He's there with Brother—nothing hurts them now. They can stand the sunlight. Ain't it strange, black men get a disease where no light can touch their skin? Ain't it so awful strange?"

"It come from Africa," Vy whispered. "Yea, way long time ago. It was a white man's disease. Traced to South Africa and a Dutch settler. Then, it became a *colored* porphyria and made its way to America probably through the slave trade."

"That long ago," Tree said.

"And all down the line," M'Vy said. "It hit our family. And you must be tested, too, Tree."

But Tree was not listening to that. Vy could see she wasn't paying attention. "When the funeral? We gone have a funeral for Dab?" Tree asked. "You will do that much for him, won't you, M'Vy?"

"Tree. Tree. Course we have a funeral."

"I know just how he should look," Tree said. "Saw it while I was with him and Brother. Dab had on this fine pinstripe gray suit. A black tie and a silver tie clasp. I think he should have a silver belt with his name, Dabney, written in script, don't you? And patent leather shoes and gray silk socks. A real fine white shirt. We can shop tomorrow, buy everything. Then, we have it in a big church, and have a silver casket . . . I can stay home the rest of the week," she added. "We should mourn him, M'Vy. He gone forever. Stay home least a month, seems like to me."

Vy watched Tree. She had stopped crying and was wiping her eyes with some tissues. Watching Tree, her face slowly pulled together. Puffy, strained, it was; but soon, it began to fill with strength. It grew tough, determined, the way Tree had seen it all her life. Vy got to her feet. She leaned on her knuckles pressed on the table to steady herself. Then she stood up straight, wiped her eyes one last time, studying Tree. Silversmith stood with her.

"I know you love you brother, Tree," she said at last. "Nobody in the world doubt that. These years, you keep him and care for him so's I could work. I appreciate that. You has been a fine, good girl.

"But they ain't gone be no real expensive white shirt," Vy said, her voice hard. "No pinstripe and silken socks. Buh-cause I ain't got no two hundred fifty, three hundred dollar to buy it."

"But I saw the exact clothes," Tree said. "It would be a sin not to buy them."

"I'm layin Dab out in that blue suit he wear for occasions in school," Vy said. "And his black shoes. I'll polish them. And his dress shirt and his black belt and black socks. They ain't gone be no church, neither. For what? They ain't but you and me, and Silversmith and Don, and the funeral attendants and the funeral director. That's all. No big deal to die and get buried."

"You sure something!" Tree hissed. "You sure do hate Dab, even he dead, you own son. Dab have all kinds of frens!"

"Name one," M'Vy said. "He the dummy they see laughin in the street, that's all. I don't hate him. I wasn't good to him when he was little, I'll grant you," Vy said. "But if it was hateful, it was because I was so young. So young! But there ain't gone be all that rich stuff you want, Tree, for the simple reason I can't afford nothing."

"Anybody can afford it once. You can borrow it once.

Let Silversmith give it to you; he seem to like you enough."

"He would give it me, too," Vy said. She turned, smiled up at him, a wan, sad smile. "But I ain't gone ask him for it. I wouldn't take it from him. I got to pay the hospital and pay for the funeral," Vy said, "and all the tests they gave him, and for opening his throat so he could breathe a little—dint do him no good. Pay for day and night nurses, round-the-clock nursing; for the room—two hundred dollars a day!—and everythang else. I ain't got no insurance to cover it, so I got to work for it. I got to pay the rent here, buy the food and buy the clothes.

"Me and Silversmith start our own catering service," Vy droned on. "Borrow money to rent a place to put our stoves in. Ain't no big deal, yet. We cater when we can, to get out from under emptying bedpans. I'm not gone never get to go back in school and be an RN. So it's gone be bedpans or trying to start my own business. It takin time. Everythang takin time. Meanwhile, I got to stretch pennies." She paused. "You better listen to me, girl."

"Sure," Tree said. "Tell me some jive. I might believe it, too."

"I could smack you for that," Vy said, "but I won't. This be a day of death."

"Of murder," Tree said evenly.

"Whatever you want to think," Vy said. "I know you hate me. I know you gone blame me for it all. Go head. But the funeral gone be in the funeral parlor. I'll get a nice casket, but it ain't gone cost no fortune. Dab be buried in his own good clothes. Then we take him to the cemetery and put him in the ground. Ashes to ashes. That's it."

"I hate you." Tree was crying now. Big tears, wetting her cheeks. She commenced gasping and choking. Sobs racked her chest. "I hate you to death!"

185

"Maybe we not be close no more," M'Vy said. "It happens."

"I'll run away," Tree sobbed. "I ain't stayin another night in this awful house wit you, without my brother!"

"Maybe you will, too," Vy said. She sighed and held her hand over her heart. Silversmith touched her face and smoothed her hair. "But I hope you don't do that much foolishness."

"I'm gone. You never see me agin!" Tree said. "I hate you both. You nasty people, you only care bout youselfs! I wish *I* was dead. I'm gone get outa here, too!"

"Tree," Vy said. Her voice was weary, distant. "I'll leave money here on the table for you, in case you do take it in your head to cut on out like a fool."

"I'm gone. You can't stop me. Can't nobody stop me. I ain't takin a **dime** from you!"

"Right. All right," Vy said. "That's all I can say. You done come up against the truth, Tree. Here's some more, so you best listen.

"I make one hundred and eighty dollars a week," Vy stated. "I spend fifty for food in this house, not counting clothing and household necessities and electricity and gas and water."

"You be glad, it's less now, Dab be dead," Tree whispered. Vy heard her but went on.

"I pay two hundred a month subsidized rent on this place and a hundred fifty on the business storefront. I pay one hundred fifty a month in car payments. All of it has to come outa nine thousand five hundred dollars a year."

"What do Silversmith pay?" Tree asked.

"He pay the other half of the business, plus the stove, plus his son's education, and a lot more.

"So I ain't got the time for a month of mourning. I can't afford it, Tree. This is poor folks' reality; black reality, you want give it a title. Dab is dead. No pretty funeral gone bring him home again. Dab is *dead!* He don't give a hoot what his socks look like. He don't care what the box look like he buried in. He dead, Tree! *Dead!*"

"I hate your ugly, cheap face," Tree said. "One day," she cried, "*you* gone die, and I'll remember this day!" She walked out and went to her room. She locked the door and put her chair under the doorknob. But neither M'Vy nor Silversmith came to bother her.

Tree sobbed as though her heart were breaking. Her world had crumbled. All that she had loved and cherished was gone, one way or another. She fell across the bed, crying, and lay that way for what seemed hours. Minutes at a time, she became still, resting. Then she would be racked with crying, hurting. But, slowly, she began to concentrate on getting out of the house.

She listened. Someone had opened and closed the front door. Silversmith, probably, she thought. Maybe leaving.

She got up, quickly taking in her room. She went to the closet and looked at all her clothes. In back of her clothes on the closet floor, she found a cloth bag on wheels. She had sometimes used it to carry a bag of groceries for M'Vy. It zipped at the top. She could fill it with her clothes. At once, she started. She emptied some sweaters, a few short-sleeved shirts and her underwear into the bag. It held more than it looked like it would. She put two pairs of warm pajamas in, and her socks, stuffing them down the sides. What little makeup she had she put on top with her comb and brush.

Where'm I to put my blue jeans and shoes? There were two pairs of shoes she wanted to take—a pair of good Nikes and her Sporto duck shoes. They were dark blue, and they would keep her feet dry in the rain. She listened. She could hear dripping outside her window, but

187

no steady rain. She took the time to open the window and look out. Misty, wet streets.

Hope it stay dry for a while, she thought. No lightning, please. Glumly she stared out. What a time to die, when the weather so bad, she thought. She choked up; wiping her eyes, she turned back to her work. Studying the situation, she found what she needed and pulled a sheet and pillow case off the bed. She dropped her shoes and her schoolbooks, papers, down the case. She placed it on the sheet and began taking jeans from the closet.

I can't take it all, she thought. But if I keep the house key, I can come back for what's left. She took three pairs of jeans. And looked at the dresses she had. She had two oxford shirts that were like new, and she took both of them. She couldn't make her mind up about the dresses.

I'll wear one to the funeral. "Which one?" she moaned. She sat down again and covered her eyes. "Where'm I gone go!" She couldn't think of one place to go. She knew kids left home all the time. She'd seen kids hanging on the street way late. She heard the news; saw the TV specials on runaways.

Whyn't they ever do some special on runaway, scared-away fathers? All time pickin on the kids. Either a drug-and teen-age–prostitution special or a runaway-kid special. Shoot. What about all us who stay and hold down everythang? Where'd Ken, my dad, run away to? I could go live wit him, if I just knew where. I wouldn't know where to begin.

Still, she folded her clothes neatly on the sheet and tied it up securely, reasoning she would come back for one of the dresses and her dress shoes when it was time for Dab's funeral. Finished, she placed the bundle on the floor by her bed. She lay down again. Tense muscles jerked, relaxing.

188

I got to calm down. How'm I gone go anyplace, if I can't think where to go? So just calm down. You got to wait, make sure M'Vy has left. Then, go to the kitchen and see about some food and how much money she leave. She say she will leave it. If she don't, I'll take what's stashed. Better take it all. I ain't no thief, but I have to have money for a room, and until I can find me a job. School. If I can go, I will. But if I work all day, school have to wait. Who'll miss me there? Nobody. Only maybe Miss Noirrette. Nobody else care about me.

Tree was hungry, but she went on thinking, planning, until she had relaxed enough to become sleepy. She slept. She awoke once, hearing a door close. She should have gotten up; instead, she slept a long while, exhausted.

When at last she got up, it was almost midnight. She wasn't surprised. She had been so tired. The house was quiet. She listened for a long time; thought she heard voices. Must have been a television somewhere. She turned out the light, listening at the door, which she opened a few inches. She stood looking out. In the next five minutes, she heard no movement, no sound in the apartment. M'Vy must have gone. Tree went to the kitchen. The fluorescent light over the sink was on, as always. It was enough light to see the table and that M'Vy had left some bills, a note.

Fifteen dollars! So *cheap*. How far can I go on just fifteen dollars?

She remembered the money stashed in back of the refrigerator and behind the stove. She took it all.

Think that's it. She couldn't recall any more stash.

I was gettin low when M'Vy come. Let's see. That's thirty-five dollars. Well, it what I got, so it have to do.

She read the note: "Tree. The funeral is Friday at eleven o'clock." There was an address of a funeral parlor downtown. She could have cried but she was too angry.

"Tree, I have done all I can. Silversmith will pick you up on Friday."

Pick me up, nothin! I'll go by myself, shoot. But you will pay for this someday, M'Vy!

Tree heard something. She pressed her hands on the table and listened. Somebody, something, doing something.

In Dab's room. No! Yeah. Yeah, it is. Tryin to walk quiet. Openin up the drawers. Who it is—M'Vy? What she doin, foolin in his room? Make her get out of his room! Tree cried inside. But what if it's Dab! Can he come back, the way Rush come back? Come to haunt me? Oh! Dab, don't do that. Don't do that. I can't stand no more.

She was shaking again. She waited until the shivering fear eased. She was weak from hunger. She stared at the refrigerator. Her head began to throb.

I'm so tired. I'm so scared!

Almost resignedly, she left the kitchen to find out what was going on in Dab's room. When she got there, the door was closed tight. There was light shining under the door; not a mysterious light at all. Slowly she closed her fingers around the doorknob, carefully turned it and flung the door open.

It was not Dab. It was not M'Vy pulling faded clothes out of two bulging shopping bags. It was not Silversmith, or his son, or Brother Rush, who straightened up, with garments clutched in both hands.

I don't *believe* it. Tree couldn't believe her eyes. "What you doin here! Who sent you here! Get out! Get outa Dab's room, you old biddy!"

Miss Ole Lady Pricherd. Miss old hag. Cenithia Pricherd who came to clean on Saturdays.

"You get outa my brother's room—what you think you *doin!*"

Tree was shaking and gasping. Her lips trembled, and her face felt like it was breaking into little pieces. How could she get the old lady to leave if she was going to cry all the time? The next moment Tree was sobbing uncontrollably, hands covering her wet, slobbery face. She was a disgrace. She couldn't do anything right.

Miss Pricherd came to her. "I ain't taken nothing. I ain't here to hurt you or nothin." She touched Tree lightly on the shoulder. Tree jerked away. Miss Pricherd persisted; before Tree knew it, she had let the old lady put her arms around her. Couldn't find the strength to stop her.

"Listen, you Muh Vy ask me to come move in here, take care of things for you. And she got everythang else to do, and work. She not feelin too good, either. Got too much weight on her. I tole her, it look good on her, but bein a little less big gone ease up the heart."

How you know anything, you old fool! Tree couldn't stop crying. M'Vy was too much for her, moving Miss Pricherd in before Dab was good and cold.

"Now. Now," Miss Pricherd said. "Come on now. Lemme take you in the living room." She guided Tree down the hall. "You ben through so much, you muh tole me how you done so much. But I'm here. I can do a lot fer you. I'm just happy to be here. I got a place to stay!"

They were in the living room, and Tree peeked through her hands at Miss Pricherd. Miss Pricherd sat her down on the couch. She had on a white apron and a white dress, and white shoes.

"How . . . how . . . c-c . . . come you . . . dress so clean?" Tree managed to say between sucking in air. Her tears were subsiding. She was moaning a little, but the tears had run out.

"You muh give this to me," Miss Pricherd said, all

191

excited. "I taken a bath in there fore I put it on. Don't worry, I clean up everythang good. You muh give me two of these little uniforms for me to wear. She say it gives me some clothes and shows the folks in the building I belong here. I ain't no bag lady. I works here and I lives here."

"You . . . gone live *here*? In my brother's room?" Tree moaned and cried but there were no more tears. She clasped her hands and unclasped them. She didn't know how M'Vy could do this to her, giving Dab's room away.

"Look. I got you dinner ready," Miss Pricherd said. "Vy have to go over to the funeral parlor. Taken the boy's suit and things. We put his clothes all in a pile in Vy's bedroom till she know what you want to save and what not."

"I . . . want . . . want his light shoes. Don't throw 'em . . . away."

"I ain't throwin nothing out, baby. We gone keep it all, don't worry bout it. Listen, I got stew and corn bread and green beans with a strik-o-lean—how's that? And that left over Chinese food . . . Lemme go fetch it fer you, then we'll talk some more."

Tree let her go. She was too sad, too weak, to care.

Taken Dab's room! Guess they be soon movin *me* out.

"Whyn't you taken my room?" Tree said when Miss Pricherd returned. "I'm leavin soon."

"Now. Now. Here. Let's have some food." She sat a tray of food on the coffee table and moved the coffee table up close to the couch. The tray looked nice. There was a napkin. There was hot chocolate and stew and good-smelling beans. And a bowl of chicken and noodles, mixed. The sight of corn bread with butter melting into steaming cracks made Tree weak all over, hungry weak.

Saliva ran in her mouth. She swallowed and got shakily to her feet.

"Where you gone to, hon. Listen."

"I be right back," Tree whispered. She went to Dab's room, to the closet. She saw that all his clothes were gone. And went to M'Vy's room and saw the pile of Dab's things in one corner. There wasn't much. She found his shuffling shoes at the bottom of the pile. Picked them up and held them close.

Tree put the shoes on, Dab's shoes, outside the living room. She let their little lights shine. Always be light on your feet, she thought, and went in.

"So that's how they look when they on," Miss Prich-erd said.

Tree sat down on the couch, letting the shoes light up when she moved. She ate the food. It was delicious.

Miss Pricherd sat near, watching her. She looked bright and alert in her new uniform. She had her hair done up in a net so that it was off her face.

Keep her face from getting hair oil on it. She lookin not so old, dressed nice, Tree thought.

Miss Pricherd turned on the TV and adjusted it to the Carson show. She didn't turn it up so that it would bother conversation. She looked at Tree eagerly. Somewhat shy now, she smoothed her hands over her uniform. She had on white stockings, Tree noticed, just the way the women in the hospital had them.

"Now," said Miss Pricherd. "Lemme tell you. Vy given me a room to stay in here. And I do everythang but buy the food. She do that or she tell Silversmith to do it. Them two thinkin about tyin up, I bet. He brang in a whole supply of food. You should see the bunch of bananas that man brought up. Shoot. And lots of good meat. I be careful. Ain't gone fool with nothin you don't want me to prepare."

"You gone cook for *me?*" Tree said. "I'm the one cooks for me and Dab."

"I been cookin for peoples my whole life," said Miss Pricherd. "Ain't the food you eatin now good?"

Tree had to admit it was.

"Well, then," Miss Pricherd said. "And I'll tell you what else. I'm gone take care of all the housework. I'm gone wash everythang and iron everythang. Even Vy will bring her thangs to me and I will wash an iron 'em so she don't have to worry bout nothin here."

"You mean you gone do it all?" Tree asked, incredulous.

"Girl, all you gone have to do is eat, sleep, watch TV and do schoolwork. Vy say to be sure you study. And no boys in this house. Well. She right, I guess. But you gettin older. They gone be boys sometime."

"How you gone do all that work!" Tree said. She couldn't get over it. She didn't believe it.

"I did it once a week," Miss Pricherd said. "Now, with me here ever day, I can do a little at a time. Cook, do laundry. It easy. I'm so *glad* to be here. And Tree. Teresa, I don't mean to be takin nothin away from you mourn your brother. Please, I wouldn't do that. I had no place else to go but the street where I been. And Vy see a way she could help you and help me, too."

Tree was astounded. Suddenly she remembered all the dirty work she had always done. Washing Dab's dirty clothes. Cleaning the hard, dirty ring from around the tub. Mopping and sweeping dirt and dust.

"What she gone pay you?" Tree said. She had eaten all the food. Now she sipped the wonderful hot chocolate.

"Don't pay me nothing fo a while, until she gets her bills paid. What I need? I'm here, sheltered and not hongry no more. That's good. I'm safe off the street. She pay me when she can, what she can. It all right with me."

Tree got up. Miss Pricherd wouldn't let her take the tray. Tree went to her room, and Miss Pricherd came in when she had finished in the kitchen. She stood rather formally in her sparkling uniform, just inside the door. "See you got all your things together," she said. "Vy tole me you might be goin."

"Yeah," Tree said. She looked at Miss Pricherd, then away. "What's it like out there?"

"What?"

"The street," Tree said softly. "What it like to live out there?"

"Well," Miss Pricherd said. She came in quietly and sat down primly on the edge of Tree's chair by the bed. She looked around her like she was afraid of messing things up. "Best you never know," she told Tree.

"You lived out there," Tree said.

"Unh-uh, no I didn't. That no kind of living. I survived. I was just lucky. I coulda been dead."

"Why come?" Tree asked.

"Well, many a time, I wake up, they done stripped me. Strip my coat and dress off. Shame! I so ashamed, bein all open like that! Taken my bags of food and clothes."

"You mean, you slept in the open, they could take your clothes off and you don't feel it?"

"Not in the open. I didn't sleep in the open," Miss Pricherd said. "They always a hall or a doorway. And you can be real sick and tired and you don't wake for nothin. Once, I had me a room. But it wasn't nothing like your room or you brother's. People see you old, they bust right in. Be sleepin and they walk in, take what you got on the chair." Her voice shook. She clutched at her hands, twirling her thumbs ceaselessly, the way Tree had seen other old people do.

"Don't go out there, Tree," Miss Pricherd said. "Young girls fall into down time, all kinds of trouble."

195

"Like what?" Tree asked.

"Best you never know. You thinkin bout leavin tonight?"

"I'm thinkin about it," Tree said calmly.

"Don't do it. Wait least till they buries the boy. Do that much for you muh. I'm tellin you, this is breakin her."

"Really," Tree said.

The rain was coming down. Back in the living room, Miss Pricherd and Tree sat, listening to it across the quiet, formal space between them. The television flickered its light.

"It rainin hard," Miss Pricherd said.

"I hear it," Tree said.

"Wait least till mornin."

When Tree said nothing, Miss Pricherd spoke again. There was a kind of hard glinting, like flint, out of her eyes. "They gone tear up that nice bundle you made. They gone tear *you* up, after that. Wait until mornin. I fix you a nice breakfast. Then you have the whole day. Wait."

"Maybe I will," Tree said.

CHAPTER
17

Tree thought of funeral homes as places you went by on your way somewhere else. She never thought she would ever have to go inside one. She had passed them on the bus sometimes, riding with Dab and M'Vy, peering out the window at the manicured lawns. But she never thought of anyone in her world dying and having to be taken to one of those places.

She stood at the foot of wide cement steps that were covered in immaculate green outdoor carpet. The steps led to a sweeping colonnade with tall white columns. The home looked richer and more stately than any church Tree could have imagined. It looked like a Southern plantation house.

"Who'd think it some funeral parlor?" Tree said, in awe. "You sure this place is where Dab is at?" she asked M'Vy. "It lookin like somebody's Hollywood mansion."

"Come on, Heart," Vy told her. She took Tree's hand, urging her up the steps. "They only given us so much time."

"They not gone run us out?" Tree asked. M'Vy didn't take the time to answer but hurried on. Silversmith and Miss Pricherd, who had decided at the last minute to come, were right behind them.

Tree saw a tall gentleman dressed in a very business-like gray suit standing at the entrance to the funeral parlor.

"He the guard? Is this some white funeral parlor?" Tree whispered to M'Vy.

"They do all kinds in this one, that's why I pick it," M'Vy whispered back. "Just you money have to be green. That man is one of the attendants. Don't worry about nothin, Tree. It gone be fine."

Tree wasn't sure. She hadn't expected the funeral place to be so grand. It made the hurt somewhat less, that she hadn't gotten her way concerning Dab. No church funeral, no fine clothes for his burial.

Tuesday had been a day of death. Tree got through Tuesday night and had not run away. It had rained on and off the whole night. There had been lightning and thunder; not even a runaway fool would have gone out in such weather, was Tree's opinion.

On Wednesday, she wouldn't talk to M'Vy on the phone. She let Miss Pricherd do the talking, instead. The old lady did everything else, as well. Cleaning and ironing, cooking. And continually checking on Tree to see that she'd eaten, that she was feeling all right. Tree didn't have to do a thing but lounge around watching the soap operas. Sometimes she would forget and rush to Dab's room, as if she thought he was going to be there. Then she would find it wasn't his room anymore, and that made her cry more than once.

When Silversmith came to check on her Wednesday evening, she locked herself in the bedroom, jamming the chair under the doorknob. "Why come she send *you* all the time?" she hissed through the door. "She ain't got one care for *me*."

He did not answer her. He talked to Miss Pricherd, quietly, in the living room, out of Tree's hearing. It was Miss Pricherd who now knew everything and pretended she didn't. Tree knew nothing. Only that her brother was gone.

Poor Dab, too, she thought now.

The gentleman in gray at the door nodded politely to them. He didn't smile, exactly, Tree was quick to notice. He did hold the door open for them; he didn't seem upset at having them there. They went inside the softly lit place. They were in a foyer. There was a young man in a dark suit and an older man, dressed in a suit, also. Tree saw a tall woman wearing a navy blue dress that had a white collar and white cuffs.

She knew right away that the young man belonged to Silversmith. He looked like Silversmith, except he was younger, not as big and tall. He carried himself just like his father, and his hair was dark and curly.

"My boy, Don," Silversmith said. "This is Teresa Pratt and Miss Cenithia Pricherd."

Don extended his hand to Tree. "Glad to meet you, Teresa," he said, shaking her hand. "I'm sorry."

She knew he meant her brother. "Thank you," she said. He then greeted Miss Pricherd.

"How you doin, Don?" M'Vy said.

"I'm doin all right," he said. "You feeling all right?"

"Better," Vy said. "Been so busy, haven't seen you in so long."

"No, Ma'am," Don said.

"We thinkin takin everybody out to lunch after-while," she told him. "They just the few of us—will you come, too?"

"Yes, Ma'am, sure. Be glad to," he said. He glanced at Tree and smiled.

Tree thought Don had good manners. He looked to be eighteen or nineteen. She found that, right now, she couldn't smile at him. She was holding herself in for what was to come.

"Will you all sign the register," the woman said. She indicated a small blue book that had a silk cover and rested on a stand. The book was open. M'Vy signed in the book, writing her name in bold black script. "Sign it, Tree," she said. "We keep it so we can see afterward who come."

"We know who come," Tree said. "We all right here." But she was wrong. There was a name above M'Vy's on the first line. Mrs. Cerise Noirrette.

"M'Vy, it's my English teacher," Tree announced to M'Vy. Tree asked one of the gentlemen about it, and he explained that a Mrs. Noirrette had come earlier for the viewing. He had told her that the family would be having no viewing.

"Thank you kindly," M'Vy told him, and turned to Tree. "Nice of your teacher to come," M'Vy added.

"Why come no viewing?" Tree asked her.

"Buh-cause I thought it would be easier on everybody concerned if we left the casket closed," said M'Vy.

"No," Tree said. Carefully she wrote her name in the nice book. Finished, she gave the pen to Don, who stood behind her. She went up close to M'Vy and said, "I want to see Dab."

"Tree."

"M'Vy, don't do this to me."

"Tree, I'm not trying—" Vy stopped abruptly and explained to the gentleman standing by that they would have a short viewing.

Tree didn't bother to thank M'Vy. Anger seemed to be her most constant feeling next to her sadness over Dab. She felt drained. There was a cloying scent of flowers everywhere.

Then the gentleman was directing them to follow him. He had sandy hair, Tree noticed. It was neatly cut and trimmed along his collar. He smelled of cologne.

What it like to know you always gone walk around in a suit every day? Tree thought.

Under her feet was a carpet that was wall-to-wall plush gold. There were chandeliers, and pedestals with ferns in pots at intervals along the hallway. There were many closed doors. They were directed to enter the one door that was open. The gentleman stood at the door as they entered. Then he closed it behind them.

At the far end of the small room was the casket. There were three tall baskets of flowers, one at each end of the casket on gold pedestals, and one on a stand before it.

Tree sucked in her breath. The flowers made a breath-taking scent. "M'Vy!" Tree whispered, feeling the sanctity of the moment. "It's all just beautiful!"

They all came forward then. M'Vy had her arm around Tree. Miss Pricherd was on Tree's other side. An attendant came, and the casket was opened. Half of the top lifted up. It was metallic bronze, as was the whole casket. Inside was a tufted, silky fabric of sky blue. Lying on the blue was the form of Dab. He was dressed in his blue serge suit. There was a dark blue velvet pillow under his head.

There was no movement, no sound other than their breathing. Tree was so close to the casket, she could touch it. She did put her hand on it. There were lights coming down on Dab. Tree knew she would never forget this moment. She would ever after remember the sweet funeral smell and would forget it for long periods, only to remember it again at odd moments. Dab had his hands in his lap. His eyes were closed; his mouth, shut. His hair was not the way she had seen it last. It was trimmed neatly.

Did they take him to a barber?

Suddenly she knew something she had never suspected. Once dead, you were no longer yourself.

201

"Don't he look nice? Just like hisself," M'Vy said.

"Like he sleeping," Miss Pricherd whispered. "He a good-looking boy."

For the first time, Tree smiled; smiled down at the casket and then up at M'Vy.

"Do he look all right, Tree?" M'Vy asked.

Tree nodded.

"It's a nice casket," Silversmith thought to say, from behind them. "Everything lookin very nice."

"I think so," M'Vy said. "You think so, Tree?"

"It all right," Tree finally said, not unkindly. She said no more.

For it was not her brother lying there in Dab's good suit. It looked hard, cold under the lights, whatever it was lying there. It looked painted; its eyes were sealed shut—were they sewn shut? Its mouth was closed tight —did they wax it closed? What it was had no sweetness of Dab, no warmth of Dab. It had no moaning, unh-huhing, yeah-yeah, sing-a-little-song, of Dab. Who put the blusher on his cheeks?

Who color his lips like that, so he look punky?

It was a lifeless corpse. A dead body. Dab was gone. Tree was grateful that he had left this weak, suffering form behind.

The casket was closed again. They stepped back and bowed their heads. Tree leaned on M'Vy; it was comforting to do so. Vy had her arms around her. Silversmith put his arm around M'Vy. Miss Pricherd and Don reached over and clasped Tree's hands together with theirs. They were all touching or holding her and M'Vy. Tree could feel their heat flow together. They trembled; they were alive, holding on.

The minister opened his bible and read. Tree caught some of it:

"The law of the Lord is perfect, converting the soul,

the testimony of the Lord is sure, making wise the simple . . . He that believeth on the Son hath everlasting life . . . Therefore if any man be in Christ, he is a new creature; old things are passed away; behold, all things are become new . . ."

M'Vy was shaking, crying silently. The ceremony did not take long. Tree knew it was over when they let go of her to stand separately. Silversmith still had his arm around M'Vy. In a minute, Don came up and took her arm. But she was all right.

"I'm all right," she said to him, quite clearly.

"Good," he said.

They removed the casket, which was on a metal platform with wheels. Attendants wheeled it out the back way. They took away the flowers, too.

"They taken it to the cemetery," M'Vy explained. "We can set down a minute, and then we'll go."

There were seats along the wall. They all sat down, not saying much. Vy took off her black gloves and put them in her purse. Tree had white gloves in her purse but she did not feel like wearing them. After ten minutes, they went outside. They saw the silver hearse pull away. It held the casket and the flowers.

Dab, you should see it now! Tree thought. "Dab should see that, M'Vy," Tree said. M'Vy looked at her sharply. But Miss Pricherd grinned. "Bet he do, too! Don't you worry!"

"Yea," Tree said to herself.

The two men helped the two women down the steps. Tree came on behind them. M'Vy looked smaller in her black funeral clothes. She had on a black crepe dress and matching coat, black shoes, black hat and a black clutch bag. Her shoulders were hunched high, as if to ward off blows. At the curb, the car doors were opened for them.

Something, Tree thought. A real, true-to-life, black limousine. M'Vy gone do it up proud.

They got in. Silversmith and Don sat on seats that had folded open.

Don leaned around to speak to her. "How you feelin?" he asked.

She regarded him a long moment. "I'm just fine," she told him. "Be glad when it's done," she said simply.

"It'll be over soon," he said.

"You ever been to a funeral before?" she asked him. Instantly she regretted the question, with all of them listening. But Don didn't seem to mind. He treated her the way she wanted to be treated, like a person worthy of consideration.

"I went to my mother's funeral," he told her. "Long time ago, but I don't remember much."

"You were just six," Silversmith said, looking out the window.

"And I went to my uncle's funeral. He died suddenly of a heart attack."

"Really?" Tree said. "M'Vy's brother die in a car crash." She did not think to tell the other part of the story. What she had said was true enough.

They lapsed into silence. They rode for another twenty minutes, then turned onto the cemetery grounds. The road wound through the lawns of gravestones. The place was the Evergreen Park Cemetery. They soon came to a halt across from a freshly turned, six-foot-long rectangle of ground. There was a canvas shelter over the grave site. There was the coffin in place above the rectangle. Tree kept her mind still, unthinking.

It had begun raining a gentle mist down on the flowers, in the grass and over them. It was refreshing, Tree thought.

Didn't it rain? she thought, remembering strains of a

song. Another one: When I've done the best I can. And my friends don't understand. Then my Lord will carry me home.

M'Vy opened an umbrella over Tree. "I don't need it," Tree said. "You and Miss Pricherd have it."

Tree walked over with Don to the site. When they were all there, the minister intoned the Twenty-third Psalm. It was Tree's favorite. She listened, feeling more peaceful. Then the minister spoke the ashes to ashes— "And dust to dust . . ." Tree's eyes blurred; she caught hold of her mind again and held on, held thoughts at bay.

Slowly the casket was lowered. She watched, fascinated, as they put the cement dome over it once it was at the bottom.

Dab, it's over.

M'Vy threw a few lumps of earth down on the cover. "It's the custom, Tree," Silversmith explained.

Why didn't I know that? she thought. Whyn't somebody tell me? Tell me the minister's name—why they treat me like I'm nobody?

Tree opened her purse and took out the one lace handkerchief she had. It was her only handkerchief. It was Spanish lace, and Dab had given it to her two Christmases ago. He'd picked it out himself, although she'd been with him. "Wanta buy that for a fren, Tree," he had told her. She'd smiled, and said "Good, Dab. I bet your fren gone love that priddy hankie."

Tree wiped her eyes on the handkerchief, then let it flutter down on the coffin cover. Tree leaned over to see, and Don held her arm so she wouldn't slip or fall. He treated her nice.

They had lunch at a restaurant called The Jade Fountain. It was quiet and pleasant; they had a table next to

205

two large windows. There was a red tablecloth and red cloth napkins.

Not any paper napkins, either, Tree thought.

"Why don't you order for us, Silversmith?" M'Vy said.

"Can't I even say what I want?" Tree asked plaintively.

"Yeah," Don chimed in. "Why can't she? We want to take a look." M'Vy stared down her nose at Don, mildly critical. But Tree could tell she was fond of him and keeping close tabs on the way he was treating her.

"Here's a menu for both you," Silversmith said, "but don't run way with yourself," he said to Don.

"He means for me not to buy the most expensive dish on the menu."

"Oh," said Tree. She and Don were like conspirators against their parents.

They all ended up ordering five separate dishes and egg rolls all around. When the food came, Tree couldn't believe her eyes. Metal serving dishes of delicious-looking Chinese food. They, all of them, could eat Chinese food every day.

"This sure don't look like my school lunch."

They all laughed. Don laughed loudest. Then they sobered, remembering the day.

Wish Dab could be here, was on Tree's mind. She excused herself to go to the bathroom. She stood in a cubicle crying a moment. But then she felt better. She powdered her face and made sure there was not a trace of tears. She went back.

She and Don stuffed themselves. He kept putting more food on her plate—sweet-and-sour pork, lobster Cantonese. Szechwan chicken, which burned her mouth, it was so spicy. M'Vy and Silversmith watched them, surprised at how well they were getting along. Miss Pricherd and

Tree had Coke to drink, and the others had beer. Don asked for an empty glass. When it came, he poured some of his beer in it and gave it to Tree.

She giggled. M'Vy went, "Tsk, tsk, Don, you devilish."

"I just want to taste it," Tree said.

"How did you know she want to taste it?" Silversmith asked Don. "She didn't say so."

"How you know, how you know!" Don said, looking wide-eyed from Silversmith to M'Vy. "How come the world goes round."

"You simple," Silversmith told him. He looked embarrassed; Tree didn't understand why.

Tree got fumes up her nose and started sneezing.

"You're suppose to drink it, not sniff it!" Don said with a laugh.

"Leave me alone!" she told him. She sipped the beer. "It's *terrible*."

"Do you think folks would drink it if it was any good?" Don said.

"Coke is good," Tree said.

"Coke is good and *sweet*," Don said. "Like somebody I know."

It took Tree a second to realize he was talking about her. She didn't know where to look and didn't dare look at M'Vy.

He's flirting with me!

"Ouch!" Don whispered. "Who kicked me under the table?"

There was a long pause. "I did," said Miss Pricherd. "You, fresh!"

They broke up laughing. M'Vy laughed longest, her high, country laugh. People at other tables were looking at them.

"Shhhh!" Tree said. "Everybody starin at us." She

didn't really care. It was sooo funny—Miss Pricherd. She wasn't so old, she couldn't catch a pass!

They had a good time. They ate and talked. Laughed. Tree went away from them into her mind. She had been going away like that all her life. She had done it at the funeral parlor. But this time, she came back aware that the people around her wanted to be with her. Don was next to her like he liked being there, leaning around her, getting closer, just to get M'Vy upset. When M'Vy gave him one of her looks, he would throw back his head and laugh.

"Why can't I flirt with your daughter?" he asked M'Vy.

"She too young for you and you know it," Vy told him.

"You better get used to it, though," he said. "Won't be long now." He winked at Tree. "I'm gone be first in line."

"Send you away to military school," Silversmith said.

Don laughed and laughed at that.

Tree loved to hear him laugh. He kept everybody smiling. And him, without a mother for so long.

Does he know about my dad be gone? She wondered. We all like a family—is it what a family's like? Talkin, being close and laughin, always knowin they there? Me and Don are the kids; M'Vy and Silversmith, the parents. And Miss Pricherd. Granny Pricherd! Yeah, it feels all right.

When they were home again, in Tree and M'Vy's apartment, she and Don talked privately in her room. M'Vy insisted Tree keep the door open. Tree hadn't even thought about closing it. Don stretched across the bed, his back supported by her pillows against the wall. She sat on the chair.

"You have a nice room," he said. "I know umpteen girls who'd have given anything to have their own rooms at your age."

"Really?" she said, but she had something altogether different on her mind. "Didn't you miss your mother?" she said, as though they'd just been talking about his mother. "Did you know that my dad left home and never came back?"

"Your mom told my dad about it," he said gently.

"And then M'Vy moved away," Tree said. "And he couldn't find her, and—"

He didn't let her finish. "Tree, that wasn't the way it was. According to your mom, she left plenty of forwarding addresses. He could have found her if he wanted to. You have to face that maybe he didn't want to."

"Maybe he couldn't!" Tree said, not even sure what she meant by that. "I'll find him and find out for myself," she said.

"You still planning to run away?" he asked.

"Huh! They sure tell you a lot more than they tell me," she said glumly.

He smiled at her kind of wistfully. "I've been through everything you're going through. Listen, you asked about my mother. I missed her so much, and half the time, I didn't know it was her I was missing. When I was eleven is when I missed her the most. All the other kids had mothers. I ran away on a bus."

"You did?"

"Just for the day." He laughed. "I was back before my dad knew I was gone. But that isn't the point. I intended to leave, but I found out you can't run away from what you've lost or what you love, either. I carried the love for my dad with me. I couldn't get away from it. I couldn't lose the loss of my mother. Dad made it easier, so I went back."

"No kidding," she whispered.

"I see you got your bundle," he said. Her bundle of clothing was still there by the bed. "I'm not going to tell you not to leave. It's not really my business. Come on, let's forget it awhile. Let's go to a movie."

"A movie—me and you? M'Vy not gone let me go anywhere today."

"No?" he said. "You wait a minute."

He went out and came back in two minutes. "Told her I wanted to get you away from here and your mind off things."

"She lettin me go?"

"Yep."

Oh, man, he taken me *out!*

"What you want to see?" Don asked her.

"What's playin?" She had no idea what was on at the movies, so she threw it back to him.

"Let's see the one about werewolves in London. It's playing again."

"Ooooh!"

"You seen that one?"

"No, but I want to."

M'Vy let Don take her car, to Tree's utter amazement, and they had a good time. They ate popcorn, and Tree was scared to death of the walking dead and the werewolves. Even Don had to hide his eyes once. Tree spent half the movie peeking through her fingers.

He took her home, going halfway around town just for fun. Then he and his father left. M'Vy decided to stay until Sunday.

She came into Tree's room. "Yo'w have a good time?" she asked.

"Yes," Tree answered.

"Don a nice boy. Glad he thought to take you to the movies," Vy said.

"He took me out. My first date." Not exactly the first. She'd gone out with Brother Rush. He just an uncle, she thought. And a ghost.

"M'Vy, I went through the whole movie and I didn't think about Dab, not once."

"You have to live, Tree; we all do. Not thinking about him for a couple of hours don't mean you don't still love him."

Tree was silent, lying on her stomach on the bed.

"I wish you'd undo that bundle, put your clothes back," M'Vy said.

"I want to find my dad," Tree said, and began to cry like a baby.

"Oh, Tree!" Vy sat down beside her. "You've lost something precious. You lost your brother and you looking to find something to make it stop hurting so much. But runnin away ain't gone do it; it won't bring him back."

"I want my dad!" Tree cried, sobbing.

"Maybe Silversmith be your dad, what you think about that?" Vy said gently.

Tree sat up, her eyes red and wet. "He may become your husband," Tree said, "but he ain't my dad!"

"All right. That hurt, Tree. But it's okay. You do what you want."

"You done did what you want," Tree said. "Movin her in Dab's room, too."

"You stop and think why I did that, too," Vy said. "To take care of *you*. To be company, to be family for *you*."

"Why can't you stay wit me?" Tree asked. "I want *you!*"

M'Vy heaved a long, shaky sigh. "All these years, I been wrong. I admit it. I should've taken less money and stayed with you and your brother."

"You can call his name, M'Vy. Name is *Dab*. Your son, *Dab*."

"I know what his name is, Heart. I should've stayed with you both. But I didn't, and now it's water under the bridge. Parents make mistakes. I did and your daddy did. I left. He left. We both wrong. But I'm at least tryin to make it right. I'm gone put it all together one day. You and me and Silversmith, and Don, if he wants, and that woman with nothing and nobody, Cenithia. Don't write me off yet, Tree."

She stopped talking. She waited for Tree.

Tree was sitting up now and Vy took her hand. Tree tried to pull away. Her eyes ran with terror and she burst into racking sobs.

"Oh, baby, don't cry so. Don't cry," Vy said. She folded Tree close in her arms. "Let it all out, hon, what it is. I know, your brother. I know how bad it make you feel."

Tree pulled away. "But what about me?" she cried. "What about me!"

"What you mean, Tree?" Vy said. "What about you, hon?"

Tree stammered, sobbing, "When . . . porphyria, *me?* When I'm . . . When I'm gone *die*, like Dab!"

"Oh, my Heart!" Vy whispered. She held Tree close again. And rocked Tree until her sobbing had quieted down. "Listen," Vy said. "We gone talk about it now." She took a tissue and wiped Tree's eyes and face. Then she clasped Tree's hands safely in her own. "You not gone die, Heart," she said. "Me, neither. 'Cause I'm sure we *don't* have porphyria."

"But what if we do?" Tree said, fear rising. "I'm so scared we do."

"Listen to me now cause this is important," Vy said. "Now. You ever have awful pains in your stomach, and backache, and pain in your arms and legs? Over and over—did you?"

"No'm," said Tree.

"Do your skin ever feel like it hurtin from just the light, or be blisters and running sores everwhere on your hands. And scars from it?"

"No'm," Tree said again. "Nothin ever like any of that."

"And me neither," said Vy. "Me neither! Don't you see, Tree? Everybody in our family with porphyria get symptoms way early on, like Dab and Brother. But Brother feel he have to hide it, who knows why. They have these emotional symptoms, too, but they don't know what wrong with 'em. It cause Brother to drink. And cause Dab to get barbiturates. Maybe first just to ease some of the hard aching. Or to calm him down so to let him sleep. But pills like that cause an overreaction on a porphyric. And it was withdrawal from the pills that help kill Dab. The pills trigger an acute attack of porphyria, just like alcohol did for Brother.

"Tree. They didn't have to die. If Brother stay away from gin and Dab from his pills, they might've lived out their lives."

Tree stared at her. "You tellin me . . ." Tree paused.

"I'm tellin you it don't matter if you and me both have porphyria. If we never take barbiturates to addiction or so over-much alcohol, we never gone have an acute attack."

"Simple as that?" Tree said.

"That simple," said Vy. "It just a metabolic defect from a genetic abnormality. The first treatment is learning that taking certain drugs or alcohol can start an acute illness that may cause death."

Tree was silent. She pulled her hands from Vy's and

examined them. There was not a mark on them. "We could've saved Dab," she said, softly, "if you only told me what to look for."

Vy sighed, getting to her feet. "Didn't ever think Dab could have it. Didn't dare. Call me a fool. Been so busy workin, making our lives—I'll take a lot of the blame," she said, simply. "I'll have to live with it."

Looking down at Tree, there was love in her eyes, in her voice, as she spoke again. "We need a doctor to reassure you," she said. "I mean to have you and me tested next week. No putting it off now. See, I learn from my tragic mistake." Her smile was worn and sadness quickly turned down the corners of her mouth. "I mean to be a good mother one day. I love you much, Tree. So maybe you might best stick around."

She left Tree alone. Tree got up and closed her door. She didn't lock it this time. In spite of everything, she liked how strong M'Vy could be. She thought and thought, sitting on the edge of the bed, her feet on the bundle. She thought about herself and how empty she felt. She thought about Dab and M'Vy's love, and about porphyria. Last, she thought about being out on her own. She didn't know, yet, about that. Maybe I will, maybe I won't, she thought. Finally she got up, picked up the bundle and tossed it in the bottom of her closet.

Later for you. I got time. Don't let nobody kick you out of your room! I don't have to hurry. My dad been out there somewhere this long, he can wait for me a little longer.

So saying, she went about her business. She washed up and fixed her face and hair. She could smell supper cooking.

What that old lady fixin up tonight? she wondered. Probably some sweet potatoes and fried chicken. Woman stone weird about cookin nourishing meals.

214

Tree sauntered down the hall, then paused and turned around. She headed toward the little room.

Opened the door on an empty, still place. There was no mystery now. She stood for five minutes by the round table but there was nothing settling anywhere.

"I got somebody else to take me out," she whispered, anyway. "Name of Don. But thanks. Thanks for everything."

She closed the door firmly and went to the kitchen. She found M'Vy finishing up one of her and Dab's favorite dishes—scalloped potatoes. She smiled fondly at Tree as Tree came in, but went on with her work.

Miss Old Lady Pricherd was at the stove. She still had on her uniform, but now had rolled her white stockings below her knees for comfort. She turned her frizzed, sweaty head toward Tree. She was honey-frying chicken in an ancient skillet she must have brought with her, for Tree hadn't seen it before.

The smell of good chicken, plus having this much of a family, gave Tree the best feeling she'd had in awhile.

And, testing, joking, "What you doin there, Granny Pricherd?" she said, putting her arm lightly around Granny.

"I'm doin it up *brown!*" said Granny. Miss Pricherd poked thin air with her left foot and twirled her fork once. She gave Tree one of her toothless grins.

And did a little dance in her slippers.

VIRGINIA HAMILTON'S books have won many awards and honors. One of these, the first book ever to win both the John Newbery Medal and the National Book Award, *M. C. Higgins, the Great*, was also the recipient of the Boston Globe/Horn Book Award and the Lewis Carroll Shelf Award. *The Planet of Junior Brown* was a Newbery Honor Book in 1971, and four of Virginia Hamilton's other books have been named Notable Children's Books by the American Library Association.

Ms. Hamilton grew up the youngest child in a large family that has lived in southern Ohio since her grandfather Perry fled from slavery. The Perrys were great storytellers and Virginia Hamilton has continued the family tradition. Each of her novels is a beautifully told story, rooted in childhood memories and perceptive observation of human nature, yet transcending the everyday. Of her work, Jean Fritz said in *The New York Times*, "Reading Virginia Hamilton is like being shot out of a cannon into the Milky Way. Sometimes just a phrase sends you off, an image or a scene, but invariably at the end of a book you marvel: look how high I've been *just on words!*" In *Twentieth-Century Children's Writers*, Betsy Hearne wrote, "Virginia Hamilton has heightened the standards for children's literature as few other authors have."

Ms. Hamilton is married to Arnold Adoff, who is a distinguished poet and anthologist. They live with their two children in Ohio.

Q

2/99